Real Feelings

She turned to the window and stared out. She heard him laugh softly. "What do you want, Catherine? Do you want me to court you? To pursue you? If that's the case, I'm not getting any honest vibes. Put-on signals but no real feelings. But. . . ."

He pulled over to the side and stopped the car. He took Cat's shoulders and then his fingers tightened in the blond, wild waves. He kissed her. First hard, so that she almost drew back in anger. Then softly, gently, so that she moved closer to him. His fingers loosened in her hair and moved to the back of her neck, trailing small electric currents.

When they separated, Cat felt tears sting her eyes. She brushed impatiently at her cheeks and sank down in the car seat. Zachary started the car and said, "I'm sorry."

Catherine mumbled, "It's all right."

Zachary stared straight ahead at the road. "Yeah," he said softly. "It was very all right."

**Other Point paperbacks
you will enjoy:**

If This Is Love, I'll Take Spaghetti
   by Ellen Conford

Between Us
   by Jeanne Betancourt

Best Wishes, Joe Brady
   by Mary Pope Osborne

Soaps in the Afternoon
   by Lavinia Harris

The Changeover
   by Margaret Mahy

When We First Met
   by Norma Fox Mazer

B the et

Ann Reit

SCHOLASTIC INC.
New York Toronto London Auckland Sydney

For Lorraine

ISBN 0-590-41862-9

12 11 10 9 8 7 6 5 4 3 2 1   8 9/8 0 1 2 3/9

Printed in the U.S.A.   01

the Bet

Chapter 1

Catherine Farley sat in class with her head resting on her arm, her blond hair falling over the side of her face so that no one could see that her blue eyes were closed. She was close to being asleep, but not quite. September was too early for school to start. October maybe, November even better. But early September was still too soft, the air still too full of summer smells and summer memories. Hot sun and white sand and gray-green waves.

Tamara Fine, who sat behind Catherine, pulled Cat's hair roughly and Cat jumped upright. She turned and glared at Tamara, who moved her head in the direction of Mr. Abel, the history teacher, who was staring at Catherine.

"Ms. Farley, if you are going to sleep in class, learn to do it with more style. You are obvious, and totally inept at charades of this kind."

Catherine blushed and was about to apologize when the bell rang loudly. She stood up and tried to look dignified; her five-feet-five of gently curved girl stood straight.

Tamara edged Cat toward the door. "Come on. We have to get to the Antique Closet as fast as possible, or all the good stuff will be gone."

"I didn't know we were going to the Antique Closet. Tamara, you have more old clothes than the Salvation Army."

"So I'm addicted. It's better than other habits I could have. Right? I want to stop at my locker for a minute, then we can take off."

Catherine pushed her hair behind her ears and said with exasperation, "You're in such a hurry, why do we have to drag to your locker? You only have two books with you."

"I need something there. Catherine, you're a grouch today, a real grouch."

They walked through the corridor arm in arm, pushing when they were pushed, yelling when they were yelled at, until they got to Tamara's locker. She opened it and pulled out a long purple feather boa and, with one graceful movement, wrapped it around her neck. Catherine put her hand over her mouth to cover her laugh. The boa hung over Tamar's sweat shirt and jeans, and the ends almost touched the floor. But the purple feathers that curved around her face, framing the high cheekbones, and green eyes, and short, sleek black hair made her look startling, which was what she was: *startling*. She lifted her chin defiantly and held her tall, thin body straight. "You hate it."

Catherine took her hand away from her mouth. "No! No. I don't hate it. But it *is* different. You look ridiculous and gorgeous. Only you could wear something like that."

Tamara slammed the locker door shut and shrugged. "I guess that's a compliment."

The girls looked at each other and smiled, and Tamara put her arm around Cat's shoulders, pushing her toward the exit doors.

They had been friends for only one year. They had met after Tamara had been in the city for a short time. She had been biking down a one-lane country road speckled with sunlight that fell through the large, leafy elm trees hanging over the road. Their branches almost met in the middle, but under them Tamara saw a car parked and a blond girl in shorts standing next to it. The girl kicked one wheel, cursed, and stood staring at it, her shoulders hunched dejectedly. Tamara got off the bike and looked at the flat tire. "Come on," she said to Catherine, "get your tools."

Catherine examined the strange young woman, taking in her feline eyes and model thinness, then opened the trunk of the car. Together they pulled out the spare and the tool box. Without saying a word, they changed the tire, groaning and wiping the sweat off their faces. When they were finished they collapsed at the side of the road and silently eyed each other . . . and they were friends. It hadn't grown slowly, it was just there, full blown, an unspoken trust and liking. As if in the mechanical act of changing the tire, they had sensed each other's directness and strength.

At the Antique Closet they roamed the aisles, trying on long rhinestone earrings, and small hats with veils, and lace gloves. Tamara bought a jacket of flowered silk and Catherine bought a narrow bracelet of green and red stones. Afterwards they went into the Come and Get It coffee shop and looked at the menus.

"I dragged you here, so I'm paying," Tamara said. "You're allowed anything up to one dollar."

"That lets out the filet mignon," Catherine said, peering at the menu endlessly.

"Come on already, pick something," Tamara said, looking at the waitress and shrugging.

"All right. All right. I'll have a Coke. I don't really feel like anythng."

"Real adventurous . . . different. Like I said before, you're grouchy today. Why?"

Cat moved the glass of water in small circles and stared at the silvery rings it made on the table. "I had a fight with Howard again last night. The same old stuff all over again. Why won't I, when he wants to?"

Tamara nodded her head. "That old one. Well, he's just a normal, red-blooded boy."

Cat raised her eyes and looked at Tamara angrily. "I'm *not* normal?"

"I didn't say that. Boy, touchy, touchy."

Catherine sighed and looked at the posters of Italy on the wall, wondering why posters of Italy were in a coffee shop. "I'm just not ready for that kind of commitment. For me it would be a commitment. I know that some girls don't feel that it's as important as I seem to. . . ."

Catherine stopped and looked at Tamara, who was staring over Cat's shoulder with a semidazed expression on her face. "Are you listening?" Cat asked.

Tamara looked back at Cat. "No. I'm looking at a gorgeous boy who is standing in the doorway. Probably the most gorgeous boy I've seen in my lifetime."

Catherine turned and looked over her shoulder. The boy was gorgeous, no doubt about it. He was tall with blond hair that curled wildly over his head and clung to the back of his neck. His eyes were a cool, dazzling blue, and Cat thought of a hot beach sky. He stood gracefully, slumping slightly, and his hand grasped the white sweater knotted around his neck.

"Catherine," Tamara hissed. "You're undressing him."

Cat turned back to Tamara and looked at her coolly. "So? Boys do it all the time. Do they have some kind of monopoly on the deep once-over?"

"Never mind the feminist discussion. What do you think of him?"

Catherine turned and looked at the boy again, her eyes going from the top of his head to his sneakered feet, slowly. Then she met Tamara's eyes and held her gaze. "He's not my type."

"You *lie*. He's everybody's type. Doesn't he remind you of Michelangelo's statue of David?"

Cat laughed. "Talk about undressed. All *he* had on was a sling shot."

Tamara was impatient. "Okay. Okay. But that guy behind you, he doesn't turn you on?"

Cat shook her head. "No. He's too full of himself."

Tamara sat up straight in her seat. "Let me understand totally. You don't like him . . . don't want him?"

"Right."

Tamara sat back in the booth and shrugged her purple feathered shoulders. "Then you can get him."

Cat narrowed her blue eyes and pushed her hair back off her face. "Let *me* understand *you*. You are saying that because I don't want that boy, I can get him? Is that what you mean?"

"Exactly."

"You mean that you feel that anything you don't *want* in life, you can get?"

Tamara leaned forward, interested in Cat's interest. "No, not anything. I don't mean if you don't happen to want the measles, you're

6

going to automatically get them. But when it comes to men, yes. If you don't want one, you can't fight him off, and if you do want one, he won't look at you."

Catherine laughed derisively and finished her Coke. "You're crazy."

"Want to bet?"

"Bet what?"

Tamara looked over her shoulder and lowered her voice. She blinked her green eyes and whispered, "I'll bet you you can get that guy without any trouble."

Catherine tried to look disinterested but she couldn't tear her eyes away from Tamara. "What do you want to bet?"

Tamara thought for a while. "The loser will be the winner's servant for a month. That means doing anything, within reason of course, that is asked of her. Clean, cook, do laundry, etc."

"That's disgusting. I couldn't *stand* cleaning your room. It's uncleanable."

"That's the bet. Take it or leave it."

Cat bit her lip and then said, "Just to show you how infantile and ridiculous your premise is, how totally without merit it is, I'll bet. I'll bet you that I can't get that Adonis, no matter how hard I try. *But*, smart girl, how do you know I'll really try? Maybe I'll do things to make him despise me."

Tamara shook her head. "A good question, but I trust you. I perceive you as filled with integrity, the perfect example of American womanhood. But there is a time limit."

"How long?" Cat asked.

"It's September 10th. I'll give you one month, until October 10th. By then, you'll have him."

"You're on. One month from now he'll be no more interested in me than he is now. I just have to meet the guy. Oh, I can see you carrying my books, walking behind me ten paces, opening doors for me. Joy! You see, Tamara, my real feelings, no matter how I try to hide them, will be communicated to that boy."

"Hah," Tamara shouted. "How ignorant you are! I'll even give you a head start. His name is Zachary Winters and he goes to Millard Fillmore High."

Tamara took out her wallet and looked at the check. Suddenly Catherine reached over and grabbed her hand. "Wait."

Tamara shook her head. "No, I said I'd pay and I'm going to."

"Of course, you're going to pay. I wouldn't have it otherwise. It's Howard. What am I going to tell Howard?" Cat held on to Tamara tightly.

Tamara patted Catherine's hand condescendingly and said, "Tell him the truth." She sat back and observed Cat's anger begin.

"Sure! Just say to the guy I'm going with, 'Don't be upset, Howard dear, I'm going after a hunk for a little while.' You are creepy sometimes, Tamara."

Tamara leaned toward Catherine and caught her eyes unswervingly. "You're not in love with Howard Haynes. You never were. He's just there. Safe. Insurance for you. Stability."

"What's wrong with that? Stability isn't a four-letter word. Or can't you count?"

Tamara fished in her wallet again and took out a couple of dollars. "It's boring. That's what it is."

Cat reached for her sweater and knotted it around her neck with quick, decisive movements. "Howard isn't boring. Anyway, is what you do any better? You go from guy to guy. You never know if you're going to have a date for a dance or a party. Is that so great?"

A thoughtful, small-girl look replaced the sure, wise one that had been on Tamara's face. "I've got hope. Every guy, every date might be one that is surprising, the different drummer, the come-be-my-love one. Howard will never be that and you know it."

Their eyes locked and Cat looked away first. "You're such a smart alec. Let's get back to business. What else do you know about dreamboat?" She turned and moved her head in the direction of Zachary Winters, who was a few tables away.

As they walked to the cashier's counter, Tamara turned and blew Zachary a kiss, which he was totally unaware of. "He works part time for Zinders Landscaping Company. And that's all I know and all I'm saying. You're on your own, kid."

As they left the coffee shop and walked

to the bus stop, eyes followed them. They should have looked incongruous together, but they didn't. The soft curves of Cat's body accentuated the graceful angles of Tamara's. Cat's shoulder length, wildly waved blond hair brought out the gleaming lights in Tamara's black brushed-back cut. The circles of pink blusher on Cat's cheeks emphasized the brown liner around Tamara's eyes. They were aware of the heads that turned, the glances that took them in, and they loved it. Tamara held her head higher and Cat moved her hips in a fuller swing, and they giggled softly to each other.

As they got on the bus, Tamara threw the purple boa over one shoulder with arrogance that made Cat, who was behind her, pinch Tamara's arm. "You're overdoing," Cat whispered.

They were silent on the bus and watched the streets whirl by. They lived twenty minutes from the center of Dabney, a small Eastern city, that was large enough to have everything and small enough to be a hometown. Cat leaned back against the seat and felt the fake leather sticking to her blouse. The bus was hot and uncomfortable and Catherine didn't like the smells of gasoline, and perfume that was wearing off, and discarded orange peel.

As the bus left the busy, crowded city, it picked up speed and soon was driving down a wide, tree-lined street that had small apartment houses and large private homes. The gasoline and perfume smell was gone and the orange blended in with the odors of watered lawns and fall flowers. Cat took a deep breath.

"I have to decide how to handle my family in this great experiment."

Tamara turned toward her, surprised. "Why do you have to tell them at all?"

"Ha," Cat said. "This is war, girl. I may need all the help I can get. I don't intend *ever* to pick up *one* of your socks, shoes, or bras from your bedroom floor."

Tamara smiled, slyly. "Be prepared to do a lot more than that. Let's see, well, your mother will think it's fascinating."

"Why?"

"She's a psychologist, isn't she? And this is an interesting experiment. Bound to divulge all kinds of human reactions and interactions."

Cat shrugged. "Maybe. I'm not sure what my father will feel. He may think I've gone round the bend."

Tamara stroked the feather boa and said happily, "It will curdle your brother Oliver's macho blood. Won't that be lovely?"

Cat laughed, too. "Yeah. That leaves Ursula. Who knows what she'll say. Since she hit twenty she thinks she's an all-purpose guru."

Tamara looked down at her red-tipped fingernails. "If things were reversed, I wouldn't have to worry about family reactions. Just my mother, and she would probably try to get the guy for me." Tamara's voice was wistful and there was an almost imperceptible tremor. Her father had died two years before she had moved to Dabney and she rarely talked about him. When she did she was obviously thrust back to other times.

Tamara stood up when her stop came and threw the boa around her neck again. She ran to the door and flashed the driver a bright smile as she got off. "Soon you'll be helping me off and on buses," she shouted to Catherine, and she walked toward the small apartment house where she lived.

Chapter 2

Catherine had grown up in the old, white house on Jemmer Street, and she knew whatever happened to her she would always think of the big, wooden house, encircled on three sides by a wide porch, as home. She had had birthday parties as a child on that porch; had huddled in a rocker and watched the sun blaze out of the sky; had cried in a dark corner over rejections and happiness; and lately had wrestled with Howard on the two-seater porch swing.

As she ran up the steps she pushed a gray, weather-beaten rocker and listened to it creak back and forth. She opened the front door and enjoyed the cool silence that met her, and ran up to her room. She tossed her books on her desk and sank down in an easy chair near the window. The late afternoon sun spangled the room and Cat closed her eyes, letting its warmth lull her into an out of body moment. She smiled as she stretched her arms and legs and then let them relax.

She jumped up from the chair and went through three desk drawers before she found an unused notebook. At the top of a page she printed ZACHARY WINTERS. Then she listed everything she knew about him: Goes to Fillmore High; works at Zinders Landscaping. Six feet tall; blond hair (needs haircut); blue eyes (warm but cool); graceful (and probably knows it); lean but muscular (probably plays tennis, or soccer, or just chases girls).

Not much to go on, Cat thought. Have to figure out how to meet him, casually, naturally.

The front door slammed and Howard's voice rang through the house. "Cat. Are you home?"

"Upstairs, Howard. In my room. Come on. . . . No, I'll be right down." No use in furthering his erotic fantasies by inviting him up here.

Howard was a few inches taller than Cat, with a few extra pounds circling his midriff. He wasn't fat, but he looked like he could use some conditioning. His hair was a light brown and his eyes were exactly the same color as his hair, as if his parents had decided to match rather than mix Howard's colors. He took Catherine's hand and led her into the living room. He put her in a wide chair and he paced back and forth as he spoke. "I came to apologize. I mean, you have a right. If you don't want . . . want . . . to do *it*, you have a right."

Catherine smiled. "Thanks, Howard. I appreciate your apology." Then the smile disappeared. "Why do you have to say *it*, Howard? As if it's something you don't want to mention. Because it's so . . . embarrassing or unspeakable. I mean *it* could be anything. Eating pizza, making mudpies, scuba diving."

"What do you want me to call it, Catherine? You *know* what I mean."

"Call it whatever you want — 'making love,' or 'going to bed,' or any four-letter word you want, but make it personal at least. Not *it*. I don't want to do *it* with anyone, and never will."

Howard stood looking down at Catherine and said, "Sometimes I think you're weird."

Catherine looked away and then back at Howard, giving him what she knew was her most dazzling smile. "Speaking of weird, I have to tell you about the bet Tamara and I have."

She told him quickly, with her words falling over each other, hoping he wouldn't quite understand what she was saying . . . but he did.

"Are you saying you are going to go after some guy? *My* girl is going after another guy?"

"Well, yes, but not because I want *him*. It's a bet. An experiment. Aren't you interested in scientific experiments?"

"The only scientific experiment I'm interested in that concerns you, you aren't about to get involved in. And you don't even like what I call it." Howard was shouting.

"Howard, be reasonable. It won't take long and then — "

"Cat. You are weird, your friend Tamara is weird, and I'm getting the hell out of here, before it rubs off on me and I begin to understand you." He turned away and walked out of the house.

Cat picked up the phone in the hall and dialed Tamara. "I just told Howard and he's upset . . . very upset."

"How can you tell?" Tamara asked, biting into an apple.

"Come on, Tam, be human."

"Okay. At least it's done. Now you just have your family to pass this by. Let me know how they react."

They would all be home that night, Cat knew. Oliver was a sophomore in high school. Ursula went to a nearby small college and managed to come home a couple of nights a week to, as she put it, "refuel."

As soon as everyone had sat down and filled their plates, Cat began. "I have something fascinating to tell you." Easy, easy, she told herself; you haven't committed any jailable offense, you have your rights, you're a semi-grownup. While explaining the bet, she spoke slowly, casually, looking from her mother to her father to Oliver to Ursula with what she considered her best I-have-everything-in-control manner.

Mrs. Farley put her fork down and looked at Cat thoughtfully. "It's interesting. I don't think Tamara is necessarily right, but it is interesting. Callous but different. What do you think, Jerry?" She turned to her husband, as she ran a hand through her bright blond hair that was so like Cat's.

Jerry Farley shook his head in bewilderment. "You're the psychologist, Pam. I'm just your old, garden variety printer. Why ask me? But since you are, I think it's a stupid waste of time." He looked at Cat and raised his bushy black eyebrows. "Why don't you take piano lessons instead?"

"I took piano lessons. Remember? I have no talent and you couldn't stand the sound of me practicing."

"You're right. You were awful. How about the oboe? Or the zither?" He looked at Catherine with a straight face.

"Dad."

Oliver pushed his plate away from him and glared at Cat. "You haven't asked me yet, but I think it's disgusting. It's what women do all the time: manipulate, deceive. It stinks."

Ursula stood up and started pulling dishes together. "What about men?" she shouted at Oliver. "They don't manipulate and deceive?"

Oliver smiled with a superior leer. "You're just mad because Ben dumped you. You can't stand that he did it, not you."

Ursula slammed a dish down on the table. "Go to it, Cat. He deserves it, whoever he is."

She swerved and spit out at Oliver, "You'll never be dumped, because no girl would be dumb enough to get involved with you in the first place."

Pam Farley looked at her children and then said, "Jerry, why did we have to have three kids?"

"I think it was so they would have companions to grow up with. Wasn't that the delusion we had at the time?"

Mrs. Farley got up and surveyed the group around the table. "Ursula, go in the kitchen and load the dishwasher. Oliver, clear the table and keep quiet. Cat, go up and do your homework, or call Tamara, or get lost. Jerry, there's ice cream in the freezer. Your favorite. I just want everyone doing something silently."

Cat went upstairs and huddled in her easy chair. The September twilight was inching into her room, and she sat in the gathering darkness looking out at the lawn beneath her. The sprinklers had been turned on and they creaked cricket sounds as they spun around, tossing silver sprays of water on the still-green grass. The smell of wet September grass made Catherine breathe in deeply and wish she hadn't spoiled what should have been a congenial family dinner.

She turned as her door opened and her mother came into the room. She perched on the edge of Cat's bed and narrowed her eyes, trying to see Catherine in the dim light.

"If you want to go ahead with this thing with Tamara, that's your business. But keep the rest of the family out of it, as much as possible. I don't want your father upset, or Oliver and Ursula screaming at each other. Of course, I'm different." She smiled a broad grin that Catherine felt but couldn't see. "I have a professional concern. I'm not sure this is going to work out the way you think, and maybe I should be discouraging you, but right or wrong, I'm always interested in how people react to different situations. I probably should have my head examined."

Catherine watched the porch lights making shadows on the lawn. Patches of grass had already dried up and the borders of fall flowers were drooping.

"Mother," she said suddenly, glad her dark room hid the expression of triumph on her face, "our lawn looks awful. Someone should fix it up, prepare it for winter, plan for next spring. Mulch and all that kind of thing. We are practically the disgrace of the neighborhood. A blight on the whole area."

"Who is that someone? Not me! Not your father; he's too busy. Do *you* want to do it?"

"No! But I've heard of a wonderful landscaping company. Maybe someone could come over and talk to you about what you'd like done."

Pam Farley looked out at the lawn, and then back at Cat. "Why this sudden interest in horticulture?"

Cat got up and sat next to her mother on the bed. "You're always saying I don't take enough interest in the house. So now I am and you're putting me down."

Her mother patted Cat's hand. "The lawn could use a little help, and I would like it to be gorgeous for spring. Sure, I think it's a good idea."

Cat bit her lip to keep from laughing. "I'll call them tomorrow and see if someone can come over Saturday morning. Will you be here?"

"Sure. Saturday is fine for me." Pam Farley got up and walked to the door. "I'm glad you're getting involved with this kind of thing. It could take some of the burden off of me and your dad . . . but let's get this on the record: I'm suspicious."

After classes the next day, Cat said to Tamara, "I have to call Zinders immediately."

She went to a phone booth in the corridor and turned with surprise when she felt Tamara cramming into the booth with her. "What are you doing? Can't I have a little privacy?"

"No," Tamara said firmly and shut the door behind her.

The two girls frantically shifted positions, until Catherine could put her money into the slot and dial the number. "I can hardly breathe with you in here," Cat complained.

Then she smiled and said, "Good afternoon.

Who is this? Oh, Mr. Zinders. This is Mrs. Jerry Farley on Jemmer Street. I've heard such good things about your landscaping and I wondered if someone could come to my house Saturday morning for a consultation."

Catherine listened to Mr. Zinders and then paled. She put her hand over the mouthpiece and whispered to Tamara, "Mr. Zinders is coming."

Tamara grabbed the phone from Catherine and, trying to imitate Cat's voice, said sweetly, "Mr. Zinders, I don't want to trouble you, since I *really* haven't made up my mind. I understand you have a very talented young man working for you. Why doesn't *he* come over, just to give me a little information, you know."

Tamara nodded, smiling as she bounced her head up and down. "Fine. Just fine, Zachary Winters. Sure. Ten o'clock will be perfect."

When Tamara hung up, the two girls grabbed onto each other and laughed as vigorously as they could in the jammed booth. Over Tamara's shoulder Cat saw Howard watching them and she gave him what she thought of as her Scarlett O'Hara smile, seductive but sweet. He shook his head in disbelief and walked away.

"Howard is a problem," Catherine said. "I don't want to lose him over this."

"It would be good riddance, Cat. Don't brood over Howard. The world is full of Howards."

"Open the door, Tamara, and let me out of

here. My brain is getting oxygen deprived. And the world isn't full of Howards."

"Well, that's something to be grateful for," Tamara said, as they fell out of the booth.

When Catherine got home, Howard was sitting on the porch, rocking back and forth in an old gray rocker. He kept on rocking even when Cat was standing over him. Finally he looked up at her.

"I don't approve of what you're planning. I think it's dumb and I think you're being rotten to me by doing this experiment, but I guess I love you, so I'll string along . . . for a while. I'll keep our Saturday night date, too."

Catherine bent down and kissed Howard's cheek. "I'm glad, Howie. You won't be sorry. You'll see, in a couple of weeks the whole thing will be over."

Howard stood up and grabbed Catherine, kissing her passionately. She pushed him away and said, "Howard. That's not what I meant by 'You won't be sorry.' Don't try to blackmail me."

Howard smoothed down his hair and walked off the porch. "Women! I'll see you in school tomorrow."

Chapter 3

Summer blazed back into September on Saturday. Catherine stood at her window at nine o'clock and watched silvery waves of heat shimmering over the drying grass. It was all perfect, fitting into her plan as if she had known the day would be hot, humid, and sensuous.

Five, four, three, two, one, blast off, she thought as she went into the shower and let the needles of water sting her into total awakeness. She washed her hair and toweled it dry until it fell in undulating waves, caressing her face and making her aware of its softness and movement. She carefully put on mascara and liner, enough to accentuate her eyes' sky blueness, but not too much to look deliberate. As she pulled the shortest white shorts she owned up over her tanned legs, she whistled in appreciation. Over them went a sleeveless yellow T-shirt, cut high on her shoulders, which matched the even, coffee-and-cream color of her legs. She smiled at herself in the mirror and kicked off her bedroom slippers. Barefoot, she stopped at her desk and picked up a large, red, leather-bound book. She held it in the crook of her arm, so that the spine of the book was readable: *War and Peace*, Leo Tolstoy. One way or the other, through his body or his brain, she was sure to reach Zachary Winters.

Cat went back to her window and looked down. Zachary was standing talking to her mother. Now and then he gestured to the lawn and smiled. Even from her room, Cat could see that he had her mother's total attention. So that was the kind he was, coming on to any woman of any age. So sure. So indiscriminate. Not that her mother wasn't attractive. As a matter of fact, she looked a lot like Cat, or the other way around. But *after all.*

Cat ran down the stairs and walked slowly out into the baking sun. She blinked as it hit her eyes, and in the moment of that blink Zachary turned toward her. So did her mother. Pam Farley in one long look took in the shorts, the eye makeup, the bare feet, and the smooth, lovely expanses of tanned skin. She raised her eyebrows questioningly. Cat ignored the question, walked over to Zachary, and smiled. Not the Scarlett O'Hara dazzler, just a soft, hesitant turning up of her lips.

"You must be the man we've heard so much

about. Mr. Zinders says you are really creative. And we certainly need *that* to do something with *this*." She waved her arm over the
grounds and looked up at Zachary, tilting her
head just enough so that her blond hair
touched her tan shoulder, knowing the effect
it made.

Out of the corner of her eye, while she
waited for Zachary Winters to respond to her
subtle but not unnoticeable sensuality, she
noticed his long legs in cut-off jeans, golden
hairs covering their perfect contours. His
feet were in thong sandals, and even his feet
looked good. Any one with good-looking feet
has to be evil, Cat thought. And what was a
gardener doing in cut-offs and sandals? In-
appropriate. Hardly work clothes. Even his
sparkling white T-shirt didn't look professional to Cat. His hair was slightly wet from
his morning shower and the damp, darker
strands of hair made the already dry ones
look more golden.

When Cat looked up at Zachary, she was
ready for the admiring expression, the
awareness of her beauty and poise. But
Zachary appeared not to have seen Cat at
all. She frowned slightly as he asked, "Did
you have anything special in mind for your
grounds?"

There is a boy who lacks humanity, Cat
thought. "Well, I *would* like our grounds to
look different. Not like every other house
on the block. What do you suggest?"

Now she tried the Scarlett smile, not quite

full force but enough to have knocked Howie over. Zachary turned away and surveyed the lawn and the borders of dying flowers. "Well, Miss Farley, you will have to really get your soil in order, make it healthy again, before you can grow anything but the most hardy and usual flowers."

Cat couldn't believe it. They were talking about healthy soil when she had on the shortest shorts on the block, in the whole town, the state probably. The boy was creepy. Creepy, but proving Tamara wrong. Okay, Plan B. Cat tilted the book she was holding, so that the title was very apparent. The gold lettering caught the rays of the sun and glinted wildly. Zachary glanced at the book and then at Cat. "You like heavy reading?"

Cat responded honestly, immediately, since *War and Peace* was a favorite of hers. "It isn't heavy, really. It's about real people, who love, and fight, and die. Who suffer. . . ."

Zach looked into Cat's eyes without moving a muscle. "I didn't mean that kind of heavy. I mean it's a big book, lots of pages . . . heavy."

Behind her, Cat heard her mother giggle. Cat wheeled around and her mother raised her shoulders in a don't-get-me-into-this gesture. As she turned back to Zachary, Cat knew he was not only creepy, he was dense, insensitive, and a bore. Howie Haynes was desirable, exciting, and of genius mentality compared to Zachary Winters.

Pam Farley pushed Cat gently and said, "Why don't we sit on the porch and try to figure out what you think we should do with this place, Zach?" She turned to Cat, "Get Zach a cold Coke and help us make some decisions."

On her way to the kitchen, Cat threw the book on a bench. "Tolstoy, we have a real loser on our hands. I should have brought out Garfield," she said out loud. She got two Cokes out of the refrigerator and sat silently on the porch drinking one, while her mother and Zachary Winters talked flowers, mulch, compost heaps. He sat in a rocker, moving gently back and forth. Finally he turned to Cat. "Do you like what your mother and I have worked out? Your mother said your window faces the side lawn, so you should enjoy your view."

Cat shrugged. "It seems fine to me." Then she silently tried to push the cloud from her mind and smiled again at Zachary. "You really are creative. I never would have thought of *anything* like what you're suggesting."

"It's just the usual garden variety, forgive the pun, scheme for a neglected lawn that you don't want to invest much money in." He looked puzzled and gave Cat a glance that said she was horticulturally a dolt.

He stood up and put the empty Coke can on the porch railing. "Thanks," he said to Cat. He turned to her mother and extended his hand. "I'll tell Mr. Zinders what we talked about and he'll give you an estimate. It was nice meeting you."

As he walked to the steps, Cat slid after him and touched his arm. She held out her hand and said, "You'll be coming back, won't you?" She held onto his hand longer than any handshake needed.

"Well, either I or Mr. Zinders will be here next week. He works out the schedules. Nice meeting you, too, Miss Farley." But he didn't sound as if he meant it.

As he drove off, Cat's mother turned to her. "*What* was that all about? I hardly recognized you, with that O-you-great-big-wonderful-man act. Catherine, do you know that boy?"

Cat sank into a rocker, and moved back and forth violently. "He's the one, Ma. The one Tamara and I have the bet about. The one I'm supposed to be able to enchant, because I don't want him."

Pam Farley put her hands up to her face and laughed, loudly. "That's why I'm going to be spending a fortune on a garden? So you can entice that nice boy?"

"No," Cat said. " So I don't have to be Tamara's servant for one second. And why do you think he's so nice? I thought he was a jerk."

"Why? Because he didn't collapse at the sight of your bare feet and curly hair, and eye makeup at ten o'clock in the morning?"

"Don't be so unsympathetic. You're supposed to be on my side."

"I am on your side. But I told you things don't always work out the way you think."

Cat curled up on the porch'swing when her mother went into the house. A stone, Zachery Winters was. A veritable, unfeeling stone. What next? This was going to be tough, and require all the ingenuity she had. She felt a moment of triumph for, after all, she was proving to be right. She wasn't interesting Winters. But she had promised Tamara she would try as hard as if she really did want the guy, and Cat wanted to win honestly, so she could really lord it over Tamara.

The vision of Tamara's piles of dirty socks fortified Cat.

She lay on the swing looking up at the leaves of the huge trees surrounding the house. They barely moved in the still morning. The quiet, the sweetness of the day made Cat drowsy, but not too drowsy to start formulating her next steps. It wasn't going to be easy, since they didn't go to the same school.

She had really learned nothing about Zachary Winters that morning to help her. He seemed so contained, so lacking in humor, and businesslike. Cat had to admit grudgingly that she couldn't hate him for keeping his mind strictly on what he'd come for . . . the lawn. She was like that when she was involved with something that was important to her. She thought she might want to be an architect and sometimes, in her room alone, she would sketch a skyscraper or a ranch house or a school, and the rest of the world fell away, leaving her alone with dreams, and sketches she never showed anyone. So Winters was just doing his job today. Okay, Zachary, round two coming up.

The ringing of the phone made Catherine jump up. Maybe he had been overwhelmed — underwhelmed was truer, she thought. But it was Tamara.

"What happened?"

Catherine dragged the phone from its place on the hall table out to the porch. "Listen, I don't have to give you a blow-by-blow, do I? That's not part of our agreement."

"Okay," Tamara said, "be withholding. What are you and Howard doing tonight? I have a date with Johnny Beigle and I'd just as soon not be alone with him. He tends toward long silences, like hours."

Cat laughed. "I thought you were the one looking for the come-be-my-love guy. Howard and I are going to Frascatti's for pizza. Come along. We'll meet you there at seven."

"Howard Haynes and Johnny Beigle. Can you believe they are the same sex as Mel Gibson?" Tamara asked.

"Don't get philosophical at eleven in the morning. I'll see you at Frascatti's."

* * *

Howard was not too happy about the double date, and he didn't stop grumbling all the way to the pizza place. "Who needs Tamara and that creep Beigle? Cat, you aren't always the most considerate girl in the world. Don't you want to be alone with me?"

Cat patted one of Howard's hands soothingly. "Of course, I do. I thought you might like a little more company. Don't I ever bore you?"

"No. Do I bore you?"

"How could you, Howard? What a silly question." Cat closed her eyes for a moment. Small lies didn't count as major dishonesties, did they?

She could feel Howard smiling and knew she had done a kind, thoughtful thing for a fellow human being. But then he asked, "Have you started on this damn fool thing with the hunk yet?"

"Just beginning," Cat said. "But you know, Howard, I don't think you and I should discuss it. It's only going to make you angry and I don't want to fight with you."

"You've never minded before . . . making me angry and fighting with me."

It was going to be one of those nights.

"Look, there's a parking space right in front of the restaurant. Lucky, because the lot looks filled."

Inside they found a table for four, shared two pizzas with Tamara and Johnny, drank endless Cokes and espressos, and tried to look like they were having a good time. But Cat was thinking of how to see Zachary again, and Tamara was arguing with Johnny about what she was wearing.

"You know I don't dress like everybody else, so why are you so surprised tonight?"

Johnny cleared his throat and said softly, as if he didn't want Cat and Howard to hear, "You're beautiful, Tam. I know that, but a purple feather thing over a sweat suit . . . it's strange."

Tamara stood up and flung the boa around her. "Come on, Catherine. Don't you have to go to the ladies' room? Your hair looks funny."

Inside the room, Tamara looked under all the booth doors to make sure they were alone. "Come on, Cat, what happened this morning?"

Cat leaned against a wall. "Well, on a scale of one to ten, I'd say I hit minus twelve. He paid more attention to my mother than he did to me."

Tamara narrowed her eyes as she put on more makeup. "Did you try? *Really* try?"

"Of course I did. If you're not going to trust me. . . ."

"I trust you. I trust you."

Cat watched Tamara lining her eyes with purple. "The thing is, I don't even know how to see him again. . . ."

"Well, that coffee shop where we first saw him is across the street from his school. He's probably there a lot. You'll have to hang out there."

Cat moved away from the wall and put her hands on her hips. "Tamara, I have a life apart from Zachary Winters. I'm not going to spend hours skulking around a coffee shop."

Tamara shrugged. "You know, I always wanted a bulky, *handknitted* sweater for the winter." She looked at Catherine appraisingly.

Catherine was appalled. "I don't know how to knit."

"You can always learn. In fact, you might have to." Tamara smiled evilly. "Because if you give up without an honest effort, you lose the bet."

Catherine went to the Come and Get It right after school Monday. She sat in a booth and watched the door closely, drinking too many Cokes and two cups of coffee as she waited. But Zachary Winters didn't appear. The lazy summer heat persisted, but the owner of the shop had turned off the air conditioning. As far as he was concerned it was autumn, and it followed that it should be cool. The front door was open, letting in the warm, heavy air and two flies.

Cat watched one fly spin from table to table, fleeing as it was swatted at each place. What a way to live, she thought, being attacked constantly, never being wanted. Poor fly. She remembered the trip she had taken to California the year before. As the plane door had slammed shut and the motors revved up, she had seen a fly buzzing around the cabin. She had been caught up by the trauma of an Eastern fly finding itself in Los Angeles five hours later. Where would it go? What could it possibly think it was doing in Hollywood?

What am *I* doing *here*? Cat thought. Why am I sitting in this coffee shop waiting for a boy I don't know and don't like? I should be home, or at the movies, or anywhere. She stood up suddenly, scooping up her books. Who needs this? Then Tamara's imminent report on the causes of the Korean War came to mind, and Catherine sat down again. Tamara had said, "if you give up, you lose."

For three days she appeared at the Come and Get It after school. On the third day, she noticed the owner eyeing her in a strange way, as if he thought she was spying for a foreign government. She'd had it, with sitting there and with Tamara and Zachary Winters.

Then he walked in. Not alone. The girl with him was pretty — not sensational, but pretty. What was more disturbing was that she looked nice, like the kind of girl Catherine could spend hours talking to about life and love and the nuclear freeze. They sat down in a booth, both on the same side, and Cat observed the way Zachary listened to whatever the girl was talking about. He was really listening, not pretending, not watching to see when her mouth stopped moving so he could say something. His eyes didn't glaze over and they didn't surreptitiously sweep over the shop to see who else was there.

Score one for you, Winters. You can tune in. But what was he tuning in to? Was she his girl friend? That was something she and Tamara hadn't thought about. He might not even be available to be interested, no matter how much she didn't want him. Well, move on, Catherine, she thought.

She walked over to Zachary's booth and said brightly, "Hi."

He looked up but no moment of recognition followed. She cleared her throat and said inanely, "It's me, Catherine Farley. You were looking at our grounds on Saturday." She felt like a fool and thought of the California-bound fly again.

"I know who you are," he said. "I just didn't recognize you without your heavy reading."

"Heavy reading?"

He nodded. "You know . . . *War and Peace*."

He didn't smile, not one muscle in his face moved, as he looked at Cat. Was he joking? Had he been aware of more than Catherine had given him credit for? Was there a brief flicker of something, deep in those astounding blue eyes? Something that disappeared almost before Catherine could identify it.

Okay, so he wasn't as much as a clod as she

thought. . . . So he might have a small degree of sensitivity. She looked away from him, somewhat off balance. Then he said apologetically, "Sorry I didn't introduce you. This is Gina Olden. Gina, Catherine Farley."

Gina smiled and put out a small hand. "Hi."

Catherine liked the quality of the handshake. It was firm and lasted just the right amount of time. Not too short to make Cat feel Gina was trying to rush away. Not too long, so that Cat wanted to wrestle her hand back. A nice girl.

The three of them looked at each other in silence, no one knowing just what to say next. Finally Catherine said, "I think I'll get a Coke. Nice meeting you, Gina."

As Cat waited at the counter for the Coke to be made, she was annoyed. That had been a totally going-nowhere encounter. Nothing gained and maybe something lost. She took the Coke and started back to her own table, but as she passed Zachary he suddenly stood up. One elbow jostled Catherine's arm and the Coke went flying all over her, and the glass sailed across the room. Catherine stood and looked with fascination at the bubbling brown liquid that lazily trailed down her pink blouse and slacks.

Zach started helplessly mopping Catherine's sleeve with the napkin he held, rubbing the Coke into it and spreading the stain. "Great," he shouted. "Great."

Gina moved over to Catherine and gently

began to wipe her blouse with a wet napkin. "Honestly, Zack, you *are* a klutz."

Catherine was speechless for a few moments, shocked by the cold wetness that now touched her skin, the fragments of ice that pelted her face, and the frantic activity that Zach and Gina were engaged in to dry Cat off.

Catherine pushed them away finally. "It's okay. Really. Everything is washable. Back off."

Zach sat down in the booth wearily. "What a day. I get to school late. I'm lousy at basketball. I slaughter my English essay, and now I drown a girl, in pink yet, with a Coke." He brushed his hair off his face and turned to Gina. "I forgot to tell you, we can't go to the movies Friday night. My parents are going out and their baby-sitter has the flu. I've got to stay home with Tommy. This is a crummy week."

Gina said soothingly, "It's okay. I'll come over and sit with you. No sweat."

Catherine thought about what "I'll come over and sit with you" would mean to Howie, and said, before she knew she was going to say it, "I'll sit with Tommy. I have no plans for Friday night." *Howie, forgive me.*

Gina smiled broadly. "How nice of you. Great."

But Zachary looked dubious. "Are you experienced? Tommy isn't an easy kid. Eight-year-olds need special know-how."

Catherine was just about to tell him he was working toward a medal for arrogance, when she remembered her motives. Keep Gina and Zachary from long, lazy hours alone; see Zach for a little while alone; and appear to be noble, generous, and good. Tamara could *never* say that wasn't honest effort. This was a bet she wasn't going to lose for *any* reason.

She smiled a slow, sweet smile, trying to ignore the sticky Coke syrup that was now pasting her blouse to her skin. "Don't worry about a thing. What time should I come over?"

Zachary remained silent for a moment and then said, "I guess you'll be okay. If I recommend you, my parents will be relaxed. They're going out to dinner. Make it about seven."

That night Cat called Howie and told him as gently as she could. "Look, Howie dear, I have to change our date for Friday night."

"What do you mean, 'change it?' Change it for what?"

"Well, I have to baby-sit. It's an emergency . . . kind of." Cat untwirled the phone cord as she spoke, and stared out of her bedroom window.

"Catherine, where are you baby-sitting?"

Suddenly Cat was aware of a body in the door of her room. Oliver stood there, making no pretense of not listening. Cat reached over and tried to shut the door, but Oliver planted his foot in front of it and leaned against the door jamb.

Catherine tried whispering into the phone, which was useless. "It's no one you know. Tommy Winters. A nice eight-year-old."

"Is he that Zach Winters' brother? Is that where you're going?"

Catherine stood up suddenly. "How do you know about Zach Winters? I never told you his name."

"Yeah, well I have ways. I'm not a jerk, you know."

"Howie, I know you're not a jerk. Look, we'll make up for this Friday. Really. Anyway, I'll see you Saturday. So long, Howie. See you soon."

Cat hung up and stood facing away from Oliver. "Go away. You're trespassing."

Oliver came into the room and spun Catherine around. "And you're double dealing. You treat Howie as bad as you're treating Winters. My own sister . . . a snake."

Catherine pushed at Oliver futilely. "Oliver, get out, will you? I have to study."

"What are you studying? Deceit? Moral turpitude? Fraud?"

Catherine looked at Oliver and frowned. "What's with you? What are *you* so upset about? It's none of your business."

"It *is* my business. It's every guy's business. We all have to protect each other from girls like you. Girls who — "

Cat laughed with affection. "Come off it, Oliver. What do you know about girls? You don't even date."

Cat reached over and rumpled Oliver's

hair, but he stepped back and pushed her hand away. "You don't know everything about me, Cat." He turned and left the room.

Catherine sat next to the window and watched the sky turn from a deep blue to a streaked purple. Stars came out and dotted the sky with pinpoints of silver, and Catherine wished she felt as at peace as she normally would have looking at twilight turn into night. *Moral turpitude, indeed.*

And then she thought about — "You don't know everything about me, Cat." That was nonsense. Cat knew Oliver backwards and forwards. She even knew that Oliver really loved her, though he would die rather than admit it.

Chapter 4

Catherine, dressed in tight-fitting jeans and a blue-and-white striped man's shirt, arrived at the Winters exactly at seven. Mrs. Winters was a small, harried woman who welcomed her eagerly. Catherine felt she would have welcomed Jack the Ripper just as eagerly, if he had agreed to sit.

"Zachary says you are a reliable, responsible young woman. Is that true?"

Catherine was startled, and began to think about it. "I guess so." She looked around the living room and said casually, "Is Zach at home?"

Nora Winters looked distracted and then said quickly, "Oh, no. He went out a little while ago."

Cat hadn't bargained for this. It was *not* part of her plan, baby-sitting on a Friday night for no reason, and the evening straggled ahead of her. Suddenly a small boy raced into the room and sat down opposite Catherine. He looked her up and down carefully. "I don't need a baby-sitter. I hate you."

Catherine stared back at him. "Wait till you know me. Then hate me."

Mrs. Winters patted Tommy's head . . . hard. "He doesn't mean that."

"Yes, I do," Tommy said firmly.

Mrs. Winters took her bag from an end table and straightened her skirt. "I'm meeting my husband downtown. I really have to go. We'll be home by midnight, the latest." She left quickly, as if she was afraid Cat might.

Catherine and Tommy eyed each other suspiciously. Then Tommy asked, "What's your favorite nebula?"

Catherine leaned toward him and said, "The Orion Nebula." Then she stuck her tongue out.

Tommy sniffed. "At least you're not dumb. I'm going upstairs. I read till eight, then I go to sleep. I don't need any help with anything."

"Don't you take a bath?"

"Not if I can help it."

Catherine nodded. "I'll make a deal with you. You don't have to bathe, if you act like a human being."

Tommy agreed. He turned to the stairs and back again. "There's ice cream in the freezer."

As soon as Cat was sure Tommy was asleep, she called Tamara. "This isn't working out. He wasn't even here when I arrived . . . and the child is borderline unlikable."

Tamara laughed. "You don't have to like the kid, just make sure he doesn't set the house on fire. Anyway, maybe Zachary will get home before you leave."

"This whole idea is dumb, Tamara. I'm bored, and I could be out with Howie."

"Talk about bored! Well, Catherine Farley, you know, I've been thinking how nice it would be to have homemade muffins for breakfast every morning. You can withdraw from this bet if you want to. . . ."

Cat sighed, deliberately. "Go soak your head. I'll talk to you tomorrow."

At nine o'clock Catherine went upstairs and looked into Tommy's room. He was asleep, breathing softly. She pulled the blanket that he had tossed onto the floor over his shoulders and left. As she walked down the hall to the stairs, she stopped at what was obviously Zachary's room. There was a small light on and she walked in. The light came from a large globe that was on a table. It was finger-marked and worn, as if it had been spun and touched for many years. There were school pennants on the wall with buttons stuck into them. Catherine smiled at one that said REALITY IS A CRUTCH. On his bureau were pictures of himself and some other boys on a camping trip. He was hunched over a tin plate of food and was laughing. A framed photograph of Gina smiled up at Cat. She picked it up and looked into the grave eyes and her heart lurched. Truly a nice girl. If Cat lost the bet, Gina would be hurt, too.

Bookcases went up one wall and Catherine looked at the titles jammed onto the shelves. He was eclectic, that was for sure. But the largest portion of the books was about gardening, landscaping, park planning, and conservation. Zinders wasn't just a random job. He cared. Was she going to have to really learn something about all this in order to make a dent into his consciousness? She picked a book off the shelf and started to read about Frederic Olmstead who had designed Central Park in New York City. She wasn't fascinated.

"Do you always snoop around on your baby-sitting jobs?" Tommy asked.

Catherine dropped the book and wheeled around, clutching at her heart. "You scared the life out of me. Do you always sneak up on unsuspecting girls?"

"I got up for a glass of water. What's your reason?"

Catherine guided Tommy toward the bathroom and filled the water glass. "I have no alibi. I'm guilty. Just curious."

Tommy shook his head knowingly. "Lots of girls are interested in Zachary."

Catherine sat on the edge of the tub while Tommy drank the water. "And what kind of girl is Zachary interested in?"

Talk about moral turpitude. Here she was

slyly trying to squeeze information out of a child. How low would she sink?

"He likes girls who aren't cute. Girls like Gina. You're too cute."

"Thanks, old boy."

At eleven the Winters came home and five minutes later Zachary walked in, as Mr. Winters was paying Cat. "Would you mind taking Catherine home, Zach?" his father asked. "I'm really bushed. Going out on a workday night is not for me."

He threw the car keys to Zach, but Zach asked Cat, "Feel like walking? It's only ten blocks."

Thank you, Mr. Winters, Cat thought. "Sure. I love to walk." She had on new sneakers that were not comfortable yet, but. . . .

The night was totally still, there was no breeze, but the air was cool. Summer had gone again and Catherine pulled her sweater over her shoulders. As they walked along the streets, an occasional sound came from a house . . . a stereo, a tv set, a phone ringing, sounds that momentarily pierced the darkness. They walked in silence, as Catherine tried to think of something to say . . . something not cute.

"Are you going to be doing something with our lawn?"

"Yeah. Your mother worked it out with Mr. Zinders. I'll be over in the morning to start things."

Catherine moved nearer to him, so that

her arms brushed against him as they walked. But he seemed unaware of her closeness. At one corner a car swept around too fast and he reached out and pulled Cat back. "My hero," Catherine said coyly. Then she thought, *too cute*. Damn.

"What did you and Gina do tonight?" It sounded awful. "I mean, what movie did you see?"

"There's a revival of *Casablanca* in town. We took it in."

"Very romantic. Don't you think?" She edged a little closer again.

He didn't answer and Catherine gave up for the night. She was tired and discouraged. This boy was unreachable. Was she going to have to go through this for a whole month? *Never*. But then she saw herself curtseying to Tamara for a month.

The next morning Cat changed her image. She wore a straight blue denim skirt with a turtleneck, long-sleeved navy shirt, no makeup, and she tried to manage her unmanageable waves. When she walked out of the house, Zachary was kneeling in a length of dirt about to dig up a sick-looking bush. Cat was speechless and then yelled, "Don't touch that."

She ran over to Zach and grabbed his arm, trying to wrestle the shovel out of his hand. "That's mine. Don't touch that."

Zachary looked at her wide eyes and flushed face. "It's the unhealthiest bush I've ever seen. It's dying."

"It's mine," Cat repeated. "I'll deck you if you touch it."

"Okay. Okay. I'll leave it to its demise. Or, if you let go of my arm, I'll try to bring it back to health."

Catherine let go and crouched next to Zachary. She touched a branch of the bush gently.

"What do you mean, 'It's mine?'" Zach asked. He sank back on his heels and looked at Cat.

"My father bought it when I was five. I planted it myself. It's mine," she finished simply.

She looked up at Zachary and it was there ... interest ... real interest. He'd been felled by a bush. One never knew.

"You haven't taken very good care of it. You really aren't interested in any of this, are you?" He waved his hand over the lawn.

Not being cute, Catherine said, "No, I'm not. Just that bush, and you're right, I haven't taken care of it. I expected it would just . . . grow."

"What *are* you interested in?" Zach asked.

She didn't want to talk about it. She rarely did, but a girl had to strike while the iron was hot. "I'm interested in building things, architecture, designing buildings."

"You sound ashamed of it."

"That's nonsense. It's just . . . private. I've wanted to be so many different things since I was a kid . . . policewoman, detective, actress

... that I just don't want people to think I'm just into something else."

"Do you have any sketches of things you've designed?"

Catherine saw the total absorption on his face. "Yes, but I don't show them . . . to just anybody."

"How about just one?"

Catherine looked away. Was it worth it? He'd probably laugh. But then Tamara loomed before her. She went up to her room and came back with one rough sketch. She handed it to Zachary. "It's a school, an elementary school."

He looked at it carefully and then at Catherine. "That's why the windows are so low, for little kids."

Catherine nodded her head. "Have you ever looked at a school for small kids? They never can look out of a window, because they're built too high in the building." She gestured to her sketch. "This way a little child can look out."

Zachary said eagerly, "Have you ever thought of building a school in a square, with the inside all gardens and free space? The seasons would be part of the school — budding branches, and trees with thick foliage, and orange and red leaves, and snow-covered branches. Every month of the year would be practically inside of the schoolrooms."

"I like that. You really care about that kind of thing, don't you?"

"Sure. It's what I'm going to do . . . landscape design. Ever been to the Jordan Gardens in Masonville?"

"No."

"Do you know what they are?"

"No."

"This guy named Jordan, rich, had an estate and developed fifteen different kinds of gardens. If you ever saw them, you'd feel different about gardens. You're just ignorant."

"Thanks."

Zach smiled. "What are you doing tomorrow? I'll take you there."

Cat saw herself sitting up until three in the morning the next night, to make up for the time she had planned on spending on a report the next day. "I'd like to go. Thanks."

"I'll pick you up at one." He turned back to his work, as if Cat didn't exist.

After Zach left, Cat called Tamara. "What constitutes 'getting him?'" She felt a small twinge as she said the words.

Tamara was thoughtful . . . and silent. "He has to say he loves you, or ask you to go steady, or give you a family heirloom. Something deep and meaningful. Has he asked you to marry him yet?"

"Not quite."

"Back to the drawing board, Catherine." Tamara giggled.

"This is very confusing. You'd think you'd want to define your terms as broadly as possible, making it easier for *you* to win," Cat said.

"True, but I'm always fair and good. I'm giving you all the odds you could want."

"Thanks a lot. Listen, want to come to dinner tomorrow night?"

"Sure. My mother has a date. I'm trying to adjust to it."

"I have to get off the phone and wash and iron a blouse or something to wear tonight. I don't want Howie to think I'm not taking pains to look good for him."

"Does he notice?" Tamara asked wryly.

"Tamara, why do you hate Howie?"

Tamara was silent for a moment, then she said firmly, "I don't hate him, Cat. No one could *hate* Howie Haynes. He just isn't good enough for you."

The date with Howie was as usual. They went to the movies, then for a slice of pizza, and then they wrestled on the front porch. Catherine finally pushed him away decisively. "Howie, don't you ever give up?"

"Catherine, don't you ever give in?"

Chapter 5

It was cool on Sunday. The air was brisk with a steady wind. Cat and Zachary went through the Jordan Gardens slowly. Zach pointed out the different high points of the English garden and the Japanese and the vegetable and flower gardens. Cat tried to look interested and to ask intelligent, searching questions, but it didn't work.

Zachary stopped walking in front of a pond. "You don't care, do you?"

"I care about the bush *I* planted."

Zachary shook his head. "A bush does not a garden make."

They sat next to the pond in silence. The water was still, silvery in the bright sun. Just beneath the surface small orange fish skittered about. Catherine took a small stone and threw it into the water, watching the small and then larger and larger dark circles stretch out from the place where the stone had hit. Like the bet. She didn't know why that thought had come to her mind. She just knew she felt uneasy and cold.

The wind was stronger and she pulled her sweater tighter around her. When she looked up, Zachary was staring at her. His hair blew around his face but he ignored it. He just looked at Cat.

"I can't make you out. Sometimes I feel that you don't really like me, but you come on a lot."

"Do you mind that? My coming on, as you so subtly put it?"

"What guy minds when a beautiful girl is giving out signals? Even if he can't figure out what the signals mean."

Maybe Tamara was right, after all. Maybe Tamara was going to win. That was ridiculous; life wasn't like that. Zachary Winters had a girl, anyway. All Cat had to do was put in honest effort for one month and then the bet would be over. The winner and new world champion, Catherine Dara Farley.

"Do you think I'm beautiful?" Cat asked, knowing she sounded cute. But she wanted to know.

"You know damn well you are. Why ask?"

Catherine shrugged. "It's part of the game. This mating game. The boy-girl game." She leaned toward him, waiting for him to kiss her. But he stood up and pulled her with him.

"I have to get home. I have a paper to write for English and I'm lousy at doing that. It's torment for me."

Catherine fought back the anger she felt. Here she was, Catherine Farley, bright, beautiful, fun, deep, throwing herself at this guy and he was just walking away. She had to keep this thing going for one month. At this rate, she'd never see him again. How did *that* affect the bet? The whole thing was getting too complicated.

Catherine grabbed Zach's arm and they stood still. "I'm very good at English. I can help you with your essay. Writing is easy. You just have to organize your thoughts." Just like winning bets. You just have to keep things organized.

"Why are you doing this? Why help me?"

For a moment Catherine was speechless. Why, indeed. "For money," she said quickly. "I need money. Two dollars an hour. Very cheap. You'd never find anyone as good as I am at English for two dollars."

Zachary started walking again. "It's a deal. I'll be at your house at seven tomorrow night. The essay is due at the end of the week, and another is due next week. . . ."

They were both silent on the drive home. Zachary concentrated on the road and Cat concentrated on Zach's hands. They were broad with long fingers. His nails were slightly ragged. She expected to see traces of dirt under the nails, but they were clean and pink. He held the steering wheel lightly, in total control of the car without any effort.

"What does Gina think of your taking me out today?"

"Gina doesn't care. She knows I'm not interested in you as a girl. I just wanted one more person aware of the green world we live in."

Tamara, Cat thought, you are *way* off. That's what she thought, but she said petulantly, "You always manage to be so complimentary. You must work very hard at it."

She turned to the window and stared out. She heard him laugh softly. "What do you want, Catherine? Do you want me to court you? To pursue you? If that's the case, I'm not getting any honest vibes. Put-on signals but no real feelings. But. . . ."

He pulled over to the side and stopped the car. He took Cat's shoulders and then his fingers tightened in the blond, wild waves. He kissed her. First hard, so that she almost drew back in anger. Then softly, gently, so that she moved closer to him. His fingers loosened in her hair and moved to the back of her neck, trailing small electric currents.

When they separated, Cat felt tears sting her eyes. She brushed impatiently at her cheeks and sank down in the car seat. Zachary started the car and said, "I'm sorry."

Catherine mumbled, "It's all right."

Zachary stared straight ahead at the road. "Yeah," He said softly. "It was very all right."

Catherine looked at him out of the corner of her eye, but he was totally involved in the car ahead of him . . . as if she was no longer next to him.

When he left her at her house, he looked at her closely, as if he was trying to see beneath the tan skin, but all he said was, "See you tomorrow. Seven."

She looked at his car disappearing down the street, watching until all that was left was a puff of smoke from the exhaust.

Upstairs Catherine ran a bath with the hottest water the old water heater manufactured. As misty clouds rose from the porcelain tub she gently lowered one leg, then the other, and then her whole body into the steaming water. She sank back and rested her head against the back of the bath tub, stretching her legs out until her toes hit the white bottom. Then she floated in the soothing, caressing water.

For the first time, she let herself think about the kiss. Catherine had been kissed before, many times. She liked kissing and being kissed. She liked the way Howard kissed her. She always responded to him, but she always knew where her response would begin and where it would end. It was exciting, to a point, but there were never any surprises. When she had been kissing Zachary Winters she had been subliminally aware of parts of her body she never thought about before. She had felt where the roots of her hair attached to her scalp, and her toes tightening in her sneakers, and her own eyelashes against her cheek. She had known the texture of his lips and the firmness of his fingers in her hair and his angular knee pressed against hers. She hadn't known the Catherine Farley kissing Zachary Winters, how much that Catherine could feel. That girl had surprised her and disturbed her, too.

Okay, Cat thought, so the guy is physically attractive to me. It happens to people all the time; someone they never thought could . . . *does*. It doesn't change a thing. I still don't want him. She felt better, dressed, and ran downstairs.

Everyone was home for dinner, including Ursula who had driven over from college to eat, get some old clothes, and borrow money. Tamara had arrived in a yellow chiffon skirt from which her dirty sneakers peeked out. Her khaki safari blouse was cinched around her waist by yellow drapery cord, and long, gold earrings dangled from her ears. Her black hair was held back by a large tortoise-shell comb, and somehow she looked extraordinarily beautiful.

Jerry Farley looked at Tamara and shook his head. "It should look ghastly. People should run from you but, you know, if I were a young man. . . ."

Mrs. Farley shoved a plate of food in front of him. "But you're not."

Ursula sat down at the table and said to Catherine, "Fill me in. What's happening with the great experiment?"

"It's just as rotten as ever," Oliver said, vehemently.

"Shut up, Oliver," Ursula said. "I didn't ask you."

Catherine was elated over realizing that a curling-her-toes kiss didn't make her want Zachary. Her eyes were overly bright, her voice too high, and she moved constantly. Touching, eating, fixing her clothes, laughing. Her mother watched her with curiosity.

Catherine turned to her sister and laughed ... too loud. "Well, there's no doubt I'm going to win this bet. The boy is not interested in me. I'm trying, really trying, but he couldn't care less."

Tamara stopped eating, her fork halfway to her mouth. "Wait. Hold it. Number one, you went to the Jordan Gardens with him today, because *he* asked you. Number two, there are three more weeks for this bet to go on. Anything could happen in three weeks."

Catherine shrugged dramatically. "Not likely. Not likely." She knew she would have to tell Tamara about the kiss, but certainly her whole family didn't have to know. For a head-spinning moment, she felt Zachary's hands on her shoulders again. Not his kiss, not his mouth, but his hands gripping her.

Mr. Farley leaned back in his chair. "Catherine, in some way, over the next thirty years or so, you will have to return the hundreds of dollars it is costing your mother and me to have the lawn fixed. The lawn was fine for all these years; suddenly it has become the blight of the neighborhood to you."

"Jerry, it *is* pretty sick-looking," Pam said.

Cat's father shook his head in surrender.

"I told her she should study the oboe. Even drums. What about bagpipes?"

Catherine laughed again . . . too loud. "You're all ridiculous. In three weeks this will be over and we never have to talk about it again."

She looked around the table. The candles in the center were reflected in her bright blue eyes, little dots of light in her wide pupils, making her look as if she was asking a question. Her mother, clearing the table, reached over and, in the eternal mother gesture, put her hand on Cat's forehead, checking for fever. Cat pushed the hand away. "*Mother*, I'm fine."

Oliver stood up and piled dishes on top of each other. "Yeah. You're just fine. Conniving but fine."

He stared at Catherine, all his indignation practically seeping from every pore in his body. Catherine glared back . . . and then dropped her eyes.

Later, alone in her room with Tamara, she said, "I guess I should tell you, he kissed me."

"Aha," Tamara said. "The plot thickens."

"Nothing is thickening," Cat said. "One kiss doesn't mean a thing."

"It's a step in the right direction." Tamara was silent for a moment, then asked, softly, "Did you like it?"

Catherine was impatient and flung herself across her bed. "It was just a kiss. Nothing special. A kiss is a kiss is a kiss."

"Really. In other words it was no different than kissing Howard?"

Catherine sat up and faced Tamara. "I didn't say that. I *like* Howard: I *don't* like Zachary."

"Methinks the lady protesteth too loudly. Cat, what if *you* begin to like *him*? I never thought of that."

"Don't worry your little pointed head, Tam. Kiss or no kiss, he still is the same guy. I never would want an Adonis type. Who needs a guy girls are falling all over, especially when he knows it. You saw the way he stood in the doorway of the Come and Get It, when we first saw him. Posed. Aware of the impression he was making. Every casual curl deliberately in place. Sweater thoughtfully knotted around his neck. Not for me. On top of that, all he knows from is gardening. Just to be strictly honest in this attempt to 'get him,' I offered to help him write an essay. Because he's illiterate." Catherine was happy to see she meant every word she said.

"So you'll be seeing him again soon?" Tamara asked.

"Tomorrow night. It's business. I'm getting paid."

"Image getting paid to be with Zach Winters. It's a fantasy to end all fantasies. Why couldn't I be in your place?"

Cat sat on the floor and smiled slyly. "You are the one who set this whole thing up. Tamara, I don't care about having handknitted sweaters or homemade muffins, but I do like having my hair washed by someone other than me, and I hate doing the laundry, not to mention walking old Mrs. Fenton's dog. How nice it will be not to have to do those things for a month."

"Catherine, you're living in a dream world. Three weeks from now, you will admit defeat in your graceless way."

When Tamara left, Cat undressed and got into bed. She burrowed under the covers and suddenly saw Oliver's face with all the disgust that he made no effort to hide. Her face felt hot, and her skin sensitive to her touch. She turned on her side and rested her cheek on the cool crispness of the pillow case.

Win or lose, what was she doing to Howie and Zachary? They were now as involved in the bet as she and Tamara were. They hadn't asked to be. They didn't even *know* they were. And Gina. She pushed the thought away and tried to sleep.

Chapter 6

Before Zachary arrived the next night, Cat tried to figure out where to work with him. If they stayed downstairs, Oliver would be wandering around, and she wanted to keep Oliver and Zachary Winters strangers to each other. If she took him up to her bedroom, would he think she was suggesting something other than working? Surely not with her parents in the house.

Would Zachary Winters ever use the phrase "doing it?" Was that the way all boys thought about something girls imagined as making love? What did it matter? And did Zachary do *it* with Gina Olden?

Catherine decided the bedroom was preferable to Oliver, so when Zachary arrived, promptly at seven, Cat took him upstairs. He stopped at the door to Catherine's room, looked around it, and then back to Cat. Her room was almost stark, with straight-lined modern furniture, vertical blinds, and nothing on the highly shellacked pine floor. The only thing on the walls was one huge black-and-white drawing of the Chrysler Building in New York City, which emphasized the black and gray colors in the room.

Cat was aware of the surprise on Zachary's face. "What's the matter?" she asked, knowing what the matter was.

"I didn't expect you'd have a room like this. A girl who is all blond, blue-eyed, and rosy-cheeked . . . and tends to wear pink blouses. . . . You don't expect this." He gestured toward the room.

"You mean I'm a piece of fluff and not to be taken seriously."

Zach smiled, very slightly. "I didn't say that. You did."

"No," Cat said angrily, "but that's what you meant."

Zach sauntered into the room and threw some papers on the desk. He pulled out the desk chair and sat down.

"Do take over," Catherine said, feeling her face get hot. Don't, she suddenly thought, don't get angry. That's not fair to Tamara. Either you play this bet honestly or get out of it.

"Excuse me for a minute," she said, and went into the bathroom. She ran the cold water and splashed some on her face. Looking into the mirror, she saw that her cheeks were red but the rest of her face was pale, snow-pale. Her eyes were wide. This whole thing was ridiculous. She could never last another two and a half weeks. She drank a glass of cold water slowly, stood up straight, and went back to her room.

Zachary was standing at her bureau, holding a picture of Howie that was in a sleek silver frame. "Nice kid," he said. "Your boyfriend?"

Catherine grabbed the picture out of his hands and looked at it. "Yes, he is my boyfriend, and what do you mean 'kid?' He's probably exactly your age."

"Maybe. I met him bowling one night with a bunch of guys. He's nice, like I said . . . and a kid."

Catherine sank into the one easy chair in the room, feeling a kind of rage she was unfamiliar with. She grasped the arms of the chair and held on to them as tightly as she could. Zachary Winters was right. . . . The words echoed . . . nice kid . . . nice kid. . . . Howie *was* nice . . . and a kid. That was why she hadn't fallen in love with him. In one phrase, Zach had destroyed all the illusions Catherine had ever carefully tried to build about Howie, all the unreal dreams, all the made-up potentials that had never existed.

I'll think about this tomorrow . . . and thank you, Scarlett.

"Come on," Cat said. "If you came to work, let's work. What is this essay about?"

Zach leaned back in the chair, tilting it on its rear legs.

He's going to break it. He's going to break

my beautiful, Shaker-design chair . . . on top of everything else.

Unaware of Catherine's clenched jaw and restrained scream, Zach said, "We've got this trendy teacher. You know the kind, he wants to show us he's one of the gang, with it. So the topic for the guys is — what is your ideal girl? And, obviously, for the girls — what is your ideal boy?"

"That's not so hard to write about. Is it?"

Zach smiled at Catherine. "I know what my ideal girl is. I just find it difficult to write down, to put into the right words. I like working with my hands, not words."

The painful, biting edge was off Catherine's anger, and she said, calmly, "Just tell me. What would she be like?"

Zachery thought for a few moments.

"Beautiful, of course. Right?" Cat asked.

"No! Wrong! I don't care if she's beautiful, or stylish, or well-dressed. I mean I want her hair to be clean and no dirt under her fingernails, but — "

"You mean like a Girl Scout, clean, reverent, honest, upright."

Zachary gathered his papers together and started to get up. "Some other time, maybe. I don't think you really want to do this tonight."

I'm making a mess of everything, Cat thought. I'm really lousing this whole thing up.

Cat put her hand on Zach's arm. "Look, I'm sorry. I do want to do this."

Zach sat back in his chair. The light from the desk lamp outlined the bones in his cheeks and the straight line of his jaw. Catherine was aware of his after-shave lotion. A strange combination of wood and sea. "I don't know why," he said.

"Why what?" Cat asked.

"Why you're doing this. I don't believe it's for the money . . . and I don't believe it's because I'm irresistible to you, either."

Cat couldn't look at him. "Then why are you here?"

Zachary laughed . . . low. "I don't know the answer to that, either. Come on . . . let's work."

Was Tamara right after all? Was Tamara going to win? No! It wasn't possible.

They were staccato thoughts that sped through her mind, hardly settling in any brain cells long enough to become shaped.

"Writing an essay like this isn't hard," Cat said. "You just have to think about what you really feel and why you feel it. You know . . . I want a girl to have clean hair, because my mother's hair is always dirty and that's my form of rebellion."

"But my mother's hair is never dirty," Zachary said with a straight face.

Cat smiled. "Tell me more . . . what else is important to you . . . and write it down after you tell me."

Zachary twirled the pencil he held in his hand, and stared at it. "Laugh. I want to laugh with her. That's important. I don't

65

want her to be lacking a serious side, but we have to laugh together."

How much did she laugh with Howard? She laughed when *she* said something funny. Howard was serious . . . life was black and white to him, and the grays that made for humor and perspective were missing.

"What else?"

Zach looked directly at Catherine. "Honest. She has to be honest . . . direct . . . no playing games."

The pencil in Cat's hands snapped in two. A small wave of guilt lapped at Cat's feet, but she waded through it and kept going.

"And?"

Zachary was in full swing now. "Bright. Dedicated to something besides herself. Caring. Compassionate . . . and sexy."

He does it with Gina. "How sexy?" Cat asked.

Zachary grinned. "As sexy as she wants to be . . . that's up to her. I'm interested in whatever she's interested in."

"What do you call it?"

"What's *it*?"

"You know, sex . . . what do you call it?" Cat asked, trying to look objective. Actually she felt embarrassed.

Zachary was surprised. He couldn't hide it. A slight flush was on his cheeks, but he just looked directly at Cat. She looked away.

"Well, if I called it 'sex,' I'd probably be part of some erudite scientific experiment." He grinned disarmingly. "If I called it *it*, I

I shouldn't be with the person I was doing *it* with at all. It's making love, isn't it?"

"I guess so," Cat mumbled. And then softly, "I hope so."

She stood up suddenly and walked around the room as if they hadn't been talking about anything intimate. "Okay, now construct reasons for wanting a girl to be all those things. Then you just organize, maybe in order of importance, and write it down. No flourishes, nothing fancy, honestly, just like your girl."

"When you put it all that way, it's like designing a garden. Just do it . . . straight."

"Exactly."

Zachary wrote steadily for awhile. Catherine sat in the easy chair and tried to read, but the room was full of wood and sea and she found it hard to concentrate. A soft breeze came through the window, much gentler, warmer, than the day before. It ruffled the papers on the desk, and Zach's hair, and it slid along Catherine's arms and legs. Finally, Zach turned around and handed her a few sheets of paper.

She read slowly. "It's good. Needs a little editing here and there, but it answers the question. Take it home with you, read it in the morning, and smooth it out."

Honest . . . he wanted an honest girl. Not someone like Catherine Dara Farley. Never would Tamara win the bet. For a moment, Catherine felt the sweet taste of victory, like honey on her lips, clinging, smooth.

Zach looked at the clock on the night table

next to Cat's bed. "Okay, it's ten o'clock." He took out his wallet and handed Catherine six dollars. "I don't think it's enough. You really helped."

"It's what we agreed to. Fair is fair."

As she took the money she heard a movement at the door to her room. Oliver stood there, looking from Cat to Zachary.

Cat cleared her throat. "Oh, Zachary, this is my kid brother, Oliver. Oliver, Zachary Winters."

Zachary shook hands warmly with Oliver. "Good to see you."

Oliver said nothing. He just looked at Cat, pain and disappointment in his eyes, and left the room.

"Talkative, isn't he?" Zach said.

"He's a little strange at times. We just ignore him."

But the look she'd seen in Oliver's eyes was not something she found she was ignoring. She had been getting used to the disgust, to the anger. She could cope with that. But disappointment was not something she had figured on.

Zachary and Catherine walked downstairs, out onto the porch. Zachary pushed the swing with his foot. "Been a long time since I was on one of these. Mind if I take a ride?"

"Be my guest."

He sat down and awkwardly started moving the swing, but his body and his feet were unsynchronized. Cat sat down next to him. "You're doing it all wrong."

Catherine started a slow, steady rhythm, using her torso and her feet with just the right amount of pressure to maintain a hypnotic, sensuous movement. They swung in silence . . . back and forth . . . back and forth. Then Zachary grabbed Catherine's shoulders and turned her to him. His mouth on hers was warm and moved over her lips. He had captured the rhythm of the swing and kept its steady motion going as he kissed Catherine and brought her body closer to his. One of Catherine's hands moved up to his cheek, and she felt the end-of-the-day stubble that had started to grow.

When he released her, he asked casually, "How about a movie or something Friday night?"

Cat paused. "Sure. Friday night is fine." Of course she'd go. Tamara should have no doubts that Catherine Farley was trying her utmost to live up to the terms of the bet.

When he left, something was bothering Catherine. What was going on in Zachary Winters' head? He had a girl. He thought Howie was her boyfriend, yet he had kissed her and asked her to go out with him. But so coolly, as if it didn't matter to him one way or the other. Was Zachary Winters the kind of guy that just added women to his mental harem, feeling nothing like what Tamara had in mind? Was she just one more conquest? Never would he say he loved her or ask her to go steady. Cat knew she'd win, but at what price? The bet had become a huge

puzzle, with none of the pieces fitting together. It was as if two jigsaw puzzles had
been mixed up, and she was trying to make
one picture out of two totally separate en-
tities.

But whatever Zachary Winters was, whatever the final picture the puzzle might be,
Catherine was uneasy. This was becoming
more than she had imagined it would be, and
she felt like a stranger to herself. If Zach
was a louse, was she any better? She wanted
to win, but she also didn't want to feel hate-
ful.

Up in her room, Cat sank down on the
floor and rested her head on the bed. She
hadn't turned any lights on, but in the soft,
purple darkness she could see Oliver's face.
More than see it, she felt the echo of his feelings in her body. She could almost *see* his
dislike of her, moving through her veins,
slowly, inevitably up to her heart and brain.

She got up and padded down the hall to
Oliver's room and knocked on the door softly.
When he didn't answer she knocked again.

"Oliver, it's me. I want to talk to you."

He opened the door and let Catherine push
past him into the room. She put her hand
on his shoulder and asked, "Oliver, why do
you hate me so? Why are you so angry at me?
It's just a stupid bet . . . a game. It's no big
deal."

Oliver's face was red, and for a panicky
moment she thought he was going to cry.

Then what would she do? She didn't know how to deal with crying brothers. But he just blinked hard a couple of times.

"I don't like what you're doing. Guys have feelings, too, you know." His voice shook slightly.

"Who said they didn't? I'm not hurting anyone, Oliver. Really."

Suddenly Oliver advanced toward her, shaking a clenched fist. "You're just like all the girls. I thought you were different, but you're not. Every girl is out to . . . you're no different. You're as mean as Mimi . . . she doesn't care, either, and — "

He stopped and his face paled. "Go away," he said.

Cat's eyes widened and she felt a shiver go through her. "Who is Mimi?"

"No one," Oliver yelled. "Go away. Get out."

Catherine walked out of the room, biting her lip to keep from saying anything more. She didn't know about Oliver at all. Maybe she hardly knew him. He had been hurt. Whoever Mimi was, she had dealt a hard blow.

Then Cat remembered a girl . . . a sophomore. Mimi. A head full of black curls. Eyes that moved from boy to boy, appraisingly. A laugh, low and sexy. A girl out of Oliver's league.

Back in her room, she saw Oliver's twisted, pained face. Oh, Oliver. Oliver, I'm sorry.

She saw Howie's brown, trusting eyes, and in spite of herself, Zach's questioning blue ones, and Gina's smile.

Catherine Farley was not used to disliking herself. It was such an unfamiliar feeling that she had no weapons to combat it. No experience. No words. She turned her head back and forth, trying to erase the pictures, but they were indelible. *Go away*, she whispered out loud. Then she groped her way to the table next to her bed and turned on the light. She picked up the phone and dialed Tamara's number.

As soon as Tamara answered the phone, Cat said, "I want out, Tamara. I don't like this bet. It's making me feel rotten."

Tamara hesitated. "Okay. You can have out. But I win by default then. You are my servant for a month."

"That's not fair, Tamara. I'll go nuts if I have to bake your crummy muffins, and knit your rotten sweaters, and do your homework."

"I knew you'd do this, Catherine. I knew you'd try to squirm out of this. But we made a bet, so see it through, or. . . ."

Cat was shocked by Tamara's accusations. "You are wrong, Tamara Fine. Wrong, wrong, wrong. I will not squirm out, or walk out, or run out. I will absolutely be in this until the bitter end."

"Fine," Tamara said.

"Look," Cat said suddenly, making one more effort to free herself, totally ignoring her strong avowal of commitment. "He kissed me. He asked me to go out with him. Isn't that enough? Maybe you were right after all."

"Catherine, that *isn't* enough. It's not enough to convince you I was *really* right. Look what you just said, '*Maybe* you were right.' Maybe isn't good enough for me. He has to say he loves you or something heavy. He's going to. I know it. I don't want you saying to me a year from now, 'Tamara, you didn't *really* win. I just gave up. . . .' "

Tamara persisted. "Be honest, Catherine; do you *really* think you lost and I won?"

Catherine responded without thinking. "*Of course not*. So he kissed me, so he asked me out; that doesn't mean what you meant in the coffee shop. 'Getting him' to you means unswerving devotion."

"Aha," Tamara said triumphantly. "Exactly. You haven't really given in yet, and that's just what I want, total defeat. . . . Of course, you can just say you're a rotten sport."

"Never." Cat slammed the phone down.

She flung herself across the bed. She knew she'd have done the same thing, if Tamara had tried to back out. She would have said just what Tamara had said.

It's only two and a half more weeks. A moment in time in the scheme of her whole life. Nothing to get hysterical about. But she felt like wailing and yelling and pounding her fist against some unknown wall. Walls were *not* for Catherine Farley, or, if they existed, they were to be climbed over. She would win the bet, and she would show Tamara she didn't welch on bets. A kiss . . . a movie . . . they meant nothing.

She climbed into bed and pulled the blanket up to her chin. She clung to the soft wooliness of it and moved it in her hand, as she had done as a small child. Slowly, she concentrated on letting a feeling of relaxation start at her toes and move up her body. Up . . . up. When it reached her face, she was aware, again, of the taste of honey on her lips, but this time it came out not from victory, but from Zachary Winters' kiss.

Chapter 7

The next day after school, Catherine and Tamara walked in the nearby park. They bought huge hot pretzels and orange sodas and sat on a bench eating. There was a steamy haze over Dabney. Indian summer haze. It drifted in the air, raising the humidity so high that the city was like a huge wad of cotton candy. The sun was hot enough to pierce through the clouds, and Catherine felt herself loosening up.

She watched a boy, about two years old, who was sitting on his mother's lap, eating an ice cream cone. A blue sunsuit protected only a small part of his sturdy body, which was slowly being covered with dripping, chocolate ice cream. The ice cream oozed over his mouth and neck and chest. His hands were filled with it. Some fell on his toes, and he wiggled happily.

"That child someday will be President or walk on Mars," Cat said.

Tamara looked up. "Why?"

"Look at his mother. Is she wiping his face? Is she saying, 'Watch out, Ralph, you're getting your sunsuit dirty.'? Is she trying to feed him the cone herself? No! She's letting the kid have a wonderful, sticky, messy experience with the cone. All by himself. That's what makes for great men . . . mothers like that."

Tamara watched the little boy. "You want to do that? I'll buy you a cone and watch you drip ice cream all over yourself, and I won't say, 'Stop it, Catherine Dara Farley, you are dirtying your pretty pink dress.'"

Catherine looked down at her feet, her red-polished toes peeking out of her open sandals. "Why did you say that last night?"

Tamara didn't try to pretend she didn't know what Catherine meant. "About squirming out of the bet?"

Catherine nodded. "Exactly. Is that the way you think of me?"

Tamara smiled. "Not really. Although, I have to confess, the first time I saw you, kicking the flat tire, I did wonder how long you'd just stand there, as if you were waiting for some man to come and help."

Catherine laughed. "Of course I was waiting for some man to come along. That's not squirming out of anything, that's just common sense. A woman really didn't occur to me."

Tamara took a bite of the pretzel and wiped her mouth on the back of her hand. "I've learned not to wait for a man to come along and do anything. In my house, if a woman doesn't do it, no one does. That's the only positive thing about my dad's death. My mother and I know how to be self-sufficient. I can even fix a leaky faucet. Not that my father could have done that. He was a writer, and writers don't know much about faucets and that kind of thing."

That was the way Catherine gathered any knowledge of Tamara's father and what her life had been like while he was alive. Tamara just dropped bits of information, indications of feelings, longings and pains, happiness and nostalgia. Catherine rarely asked direct questions, knowing Tamara preferred to offer what she wanted to, when she wanted to.

"I did think you wouldn't want to see this bet through. That if things got uncomfortable, you'd change your mind. Nobody likes to be uncomfortable . . . nothing wrong with that. You're the one that's got the load in this thing. I just watch."

"Well, don't worry. I'm just as committed to this as you are. Unless *you* want to squirm out. After all, I'm going to make you look pretty silly. Maybe you'd rather give in now."

"Nuts to you, girl. When are you seeing him again?"

"Friday. We're going to a movie . . . or something," Cat said.

Tamara turned to Catherine. "Why didn't you mention that before? Trying to hide important pieces of evidence? I'm going to win, Cat. No doubt."

Catherine stood up, brushing crumbs off her denim skirt. "We made this bet two weeks ago. If in the next two weeks the guy doesn't fall at my feet, I am the victor. I'm doing my share. I am working hard at this, and so far, dear girl, I don't have him. Not by the definition *you* made."

Tamara stood up, too. "Catherine, empires have fallen in two weeks, and so can Zachary Winters."

They started walking out of the park slowly. Catherine picked at the leaves of bushes she brushed past. "Tamara, I think if you were in my place, you'd find it made you feel crummy . . . sneaky, underhanded — a witness for the prosecution."

"You're squirming, Catherine. Trying to play on my soft feelings."

Catherine didn't answer.

Tamara put her arm around Cat's shoulders. "Want to come home with me for dinner? My mom is going to be out tonight. I wouldn't mind some company."

"Me in particular?" Cat asked. "Or just any warm body?"

Tamara squeezed Catherine's shoulder. "You in particular."

Tamara and her mother lived in a small apartment house near the Farleys. The apartment was cool and dark when the girls walked into it. The blinds had been drawn to keep the afternoon sun out, and as Tamara walked from room to room pulling them up, sunlight flooded the large, airy rooms. Tamara's bedroom was like Tamara. Bright necklaces and multicolored boas and flowered scarves hung from hooks along the walls. Hats were clinging to painted nails that had been hammered into one red wall. There was color everywhere, in the bedspread and the shag rug on the floor. In the posters and prints tacked up and in the blinds on the windows.

Catherine stretched out on the floor, while Tamara threw herself into a chair.

"Where's your mother going tonight?" Cat asked. "Date?"

Tamara shook her head. "No. She's taking a course called, Getting the Most Out of Single Living."

Cat sat up. "What do they teach her? Sex education?"

Tamara laughed and slouched further down in the chair. "I don't know, but last week, the night after her class, she set the table with our best dishes and glasses. It seems you're not supposed to eat off of paper plates just because there's no man around — or woman, as the case may be. You're suppose to treat yourself like a guest."

"Makes sense," Cat said.

"Yeah?" Tamara asked. "The only problem was, Mother wouldn't put all the good stuff in the dishwasher, so we had to stand there doing everything by hand. I felt like a pilgrim."

Tamara suddenly became serious. "I shouldn't joke about her. She's doing really well, since she's been alone. She's gotten two promotions in a year. She's now the one and only office manager at George's Hat Company. . . . But I hear her sometimes late at night, crying. I guess she hears me, too, sometimes . . . crying."

"I'm sorry," Catherine said softly.

"That's why I thought you might try to get out of the bet. I'm used to being uncomfortable . . . you're not. That's why you cling to Howie. It's comfortable."

Cat didn't answer. But she knew it was true. So true that she had to close her eyes for a moment to try to escape it.

They took two pizzas out of the freezer, and over dinner Cat said, "This whole thing is very confusing to me, Tamara. I can't figure Winters out. One minute I think he's a nice, open guy, and the next I think he's a louse."

"He's probably both."

Cat stopped eating and looked at Tam. "You make these broad, sweeping statements, and sometimes I think you *know* you don't know what you're talking about."

"Of course. I'm only sixteen. I'm not supposed to know everything . . . just think I do."

Catherine snorted.

"Anyway," Tamara went on, "it doesn't

matter what Winters is. It has nothing to do with the outcome. . . . If you don't want him, louse or not, you'll get him."

Cat nibbled on a slice of pizza and drank some Coke. "Don't *you* feel this has gotten complicated? That what seemed so simple in the beginning, isn't so simple anymore?"

Tamara licked her fingers and then went to the sink to wash them off. "No. You see, I'm just the observer . . . the commentator. . . . I don't have to do anything except make sure *you* are working hard at this. That you're not meeting him in ugly clothes, needing a bath, and then being nasty and unappealing. As long as you're playing fair, I just sit back and wait."

Catherine laughed wistfully. "I'm playing fair. I don't know why, but I am. I mean, why is it more important to be fair to you than to Zachary and Howie?"

"Because we're women together in a man's world," Tamara joked.

"Don't laugh. Maybe that's a part of it somewhere. Making things more confusing."

On Thursday night, Zachary called Catherine. She had just about decided that he had forgotten about their date, and was feeling a great sense of relief, when the phone rang.

"Do you like amusement parks?" he asked.

"I can take them or leave them," Cat answered.

"Okay, take them tomorrow night. You'll love it."

"I'm not so sure," Cat answered. She started brushing her hair with one hand, as she held the receiver with the other. Amusement park. How infantile could he get? But she had to be pleasant about it. "I'm sure it will be fine . . . I mean *great fun*." How you lie, she thought.

"I'll pick you up at seven-thirty. Casual clothes and bring a sweater. It gets cool out there at night."

"See you," Cat answered. She hung up and stared out of the window. How many guys would think to tell a girl to bring a sweater? Not many. It touched her. Zachary Winters was such a strange combination of thoughtfulness and callousness. Bring a sweater, but the hell with Gina.

It was warm Friday night, so warm that Catherine was looking forward to Joytime Park as much as she would to going into a sauna. But when Zachary arrived, she smiled and pretended that nothing would please her more than a hot, sticky, noisy amusement park. In his car, she suddenly found she had nothing to say to him. The silence was awkward and made Cat uncomfortable. Say something, idiot. Be scintillating or Tamara will give you demerits for lacking in communication.

"It's hot. Isn't it?" Cat said, trying to make the stiff statement sound meaningful.

"Yeah," Zach replied.

Deliver me. Catherine twisted in her seat, wondering if it would be odd if she suddenly opened the door and stepped out of the moving car.

Then Zachary said, "You don't have to talk, you know. There's nothing wrong with silence, if you have nothing you want to say."

"Please, don't lecture me. I know how to behave on a date." Now I've gotten demerits for surliness.

Zachary smiled. "Sorry. I was just trying to make conversation."

They laughed then, and Catherine felt at ease. Particularly at ease, since Howie was at his grandmother's birthday party and she hadn't had to break a date with him to be with Zachary.

At Joytime, Zachary said firmly, "I want you to know right from the start, I don't go on the roller coaster, the parachute jump, or anything like that."

"Why not?" Cat asked.

"Why not? Why not? Because they scare the daylights out of me. Anything wrong with that?"

"It's okay with me. I have no particular desire to throw up too early in the evening."

Zachary took Catherine's hand, as they fought their way through crowds of pushing teenagers, crying children, irritated parents, and even some people who seemed to be having a good time.

"Are you planning on throwing up this evening?" Zach asked nervously.

Catherine laughed at the panic in his voice. "Not really. Relax."

It was getting dark and the lights in the park cut through the purple dusk. Red and green and yellow slashes of color touched the people walking around, making them look wonderfully clownish. The air was filled with the odors of hot dogs and popcorn and chocolate syrup. And the sounds of laughter and music and barkers. It was hot, but a breeze blew off the nearby lake, giving the night air movement.

"That," Catherine shouted, pointing to the merry-go-round. "Is that tame enough for you?"

"Right up my alley," Zach replied. "Anything that a three-year-old can take, I can."

He walked to the ticket window and took out his wallet. Catherine put her hand on his arm. "Look, this is dutch. I mean these simple bring-the-family parks can cost a lot."

"Don't worry. If I go bankrupt before the end of the night, I'll let you know."

As they stepped on the carousel platform, Zach asked, "What's your preference? Wild horses, swans, gentle mares? Name it."

"That one. Absolutely that one." Cat waved her arm at a huge black horse, whose mouth was open in what must have been a threatening neigh, and who had a flying mane of black hair. Zach helped her up on it and jumped onto the red horse that was next to it.

As the merry-go-round gathered speed, Catherine rested her head against the pole attached to her horse. As it went up and down, Cat shouted, "Go. Go. Go."

Zachary whooped loudly as he spun around, and reached frantically for the brass rings he passed. Finally, he grabbed one and flourished it in the air triumphantly. When they got off the carousel, he handed the ring to Catherine. "For you."

Catherine took it and put it in the pocket of her jeans. "My mother always told me not to accept expensive gifts from gentlemen, but in this case. . . ."

"Are you hungry?" Zach asked, as they passed a hot dog stand.

Catherine nodded yes. "But not for hot dogs. I know it's un-American, but I don't like them."

"Aha," Zach said. "But you've never had a Winters' specialty. You won't be able to resist it."

"I think I can." Then she heard Tamara's voice: *Cooperate.* "Sure, I'll have one."

He bought two hot dogs and then proceeded to pile each one with mustard, ketchup, relish, sauerkraut, and crumbled potato chips. He handed one to her and she looked at it dubiously. As she bit into it, Zachary watched her face carefully.

"Like it?"

Catherine grimaced. "Honestly?"

"Honestly."

"It's awful."

Zachary looked pained and reached for the frankfurter in Cat's hand. "No! No!" Cat cried out. "It's awful, but interesting. I'll eat it." And die in the process, probably.

They roamed over the park, driving the dodge-em cars, clinging to each other on the ferris wheel, stuffing themselves with cotton candy and popcorn and ice cream, until Catherine thought her earlier joke about throwing up might have had more truth in it than she'd realized. Zach bought her a bright red balloon and they sat down on a bench to to rest.

"Look at this place. What do they call it?" he asked.

"What do you mean? It's called Joytime."

"Joytime what?" he persisted.

"Joytime Park," Cat answered.

"Exactly. Park. But look around you. Do you see one tree? Just one."

"You're right. But I have to tell you, there are some behind the ladies' room."

Zach laughed. "That's something . . . if you're a lady."

He took Cat's hand and pulled her off the bench. "Last event for the evening, I pick. Tunnel of Love. Okay with you?"

Cat walked alongside of him and for a brief moment she thought of Gina. "Sure. It's fine with me."

As they pushed their way to the tunnel, Zach asked, "Are you having a good time, Catherine? I know you didn't really want to come here."

Catherine looked up at him, noting the total sincerity on his face. On one of his two faces, anyway. Obviously he was a scheming, two-faced boy, but she was — she was having a wonderful time. "I am. I really am having a good time."

She had felt free, been happy, laughed. Even if Zachary Winters was untrustworthy and disreputable, it was a joyous night.

In the Tunnel of Love, he put his arm around her shoulders and drew her to him. But that was all. As they rode through the dark tunnel and reacted violently and properly to all the surprises, she waited for him to kiss her. But he didn't. She wondered what Tamara would expect of her in a situation like this. Take the initiative and kiss him passionately? Well, *she* wouldn't.

But she did rest her head on his shoulder and he let his cheek touch her soft hair . . . but just for a moment.

You are beyond understanding, Cat cried silently.

After the Tunnel of Love, they walked to the parking lot holding hands. As he pulled out of the space, Zach said, "I know a nice way to get home, staying off the highway. Are you afraid of dark, lonely, twisting country roads?"

"You make it sound like a Gothic novel."

"Not quite. You'll see."

Soon they were driving down just what Zach had described, a dark, lonely, twisting road. The night was perfectly still, no sounds except crickets. No lights except the headlights of Zach's car. The air was much cooler than in the park and it held a dampness that Cat liked. It was like being in the center of a mass of black cotton — soft, strange, pervasive. Suddenly the car began making coughing sounds and it jerked along the road, finally stopping.

"What happened?" Cat asked, nervously.

Zack shook his head. "You're not going to believe this, but we're out of gas."

Cat pulled her sweater tighter around her and stared straight ahead. "You're right! I don't believe you. *That* is the oldest trick in the world. You take a girl to a deserted, dark, out of the way place, and then you say you're out of gas. How dumb do you think I am?"

Zach took her head in his hands and turned it toward the dashboard. "Look at the dashboard. Look at the gas indicator. What does it read?"

Cat looked at it. "It reads E for empty. But don't tell me you didn't plan this. How convenient that you ran out here. How come it didn't happen in the parking lot or when we passed that gas station on the way?"

Cat was angry and hurt and disappointed. Angry that Zachary had done this to her. Hurt that he thought she was so stupid that she would believe him. Disappointed because he was a conniving, manipulative boy.

"Catherine, I did *not* plan this. I didn't check the gas before I left. That was dumb, but not deliberate."

"I still don't believe you, but now what do we do? We're hardly on any commercial artery. No one is going to come along here until morning. Maybe not ever."

Zach opened his door. "Well, I'm going to walk back to that gas station. I know the guys that work there. One of them will drive me back here with enough gas to get us back to the station. Come on, let's go."

Catherine huddled in the corner of the car. "I'm not going! It's at least three miles back to the station. It's dark and I don't trust you or what might be out there."

Zach got out of the car and walked over to Catherine's side. "Okay, then you can stay here and wait until I get back."

Catherine swung the door open and got out of the car. "Are you crazy? I'm not staying here alone. You're really rotten, Zachary Winters. Thoughtless, deceitful, and rotten."

Zachary stood still in the road. "Catherine, you can stay, you can come. One or the other. Make your choice."

"You know damn well I'm going to come. Do you think I'm going to sit in that car and wait to be attacked?"

Zach grinned. "I thought you said no one was going to come along this road."

"Oh, shut up," Cat said. "How are we going to see where we're going? It's so dark I can hardly see where *you* are."

Zach went back to the car and went through the glove compartment, until he found a flashlight. "Behold. A star to light our way."

He started out and Catherine trudged behind him, not wanting to walk next to him. The country night sounds were all around her — soft rustles of leaves, birds calling, small animals scrambling in the woods around her. She looked at Zachary's straight, muscular back. He looked so upright, so dependable, and he was so untrustworthy. She knew he had planned on their spending a few cozy hours in the car. If she had shown the slightest interest in playing little love games in the backseat, he woud have made his first move. A tear wandered down her cheek and she furiously brushed it away.

They walked for what seemed like hours. Catherine grumbled constantly, about macho boys and lies and the darkness and, finally, feet that hurt too much to move another step.

Zachary stopped walking and bent over slightly. "Okay. Okay. Get on board. I'll piggyback you for a while."

Catherine retreated a few steps. "Absolutely not! Do you think I'm a child to be carried on your back? Or a helpless female that you can talk about tomorrow to your buddies? Do you think you're so strong and I'm so weak?"

Zachary sighed. "Cat, I'm trying to make up for my mistake. I'm trying to help you. And you are being obtuse, unpleasant, and nasty."

It was the word nasty. It floated in the air, surrounding Catherine. "That you're not meeting him in ugly clothes, needing a bath, and then being nasty and unappealing." That was what Tamara had said. Cat did a mental checklist. Her clothes were okay, she didn't need a bath. But nasty and unappealing? She rated high on the last two. So how is she going to find out? Cat asked herself. No way, unless you tell her. Then you'll lose the bet. No doubt Tamara will say you didn't try.

Catherine felt another tear drip down her cheek. She was lying to Zachary, and to Howie; she was destructive to Gina, she had lost Oliver's respect. No way could she lie to Tamara, too. If it took every last bit of moral strength she had, she would be straight with Tamara. And lose the bet. Tamara would say this had been a perfect opportunity to show what a considerate girl Cat was, what a good sport, what a caring, forgiving nature she had.

Catherine looked at Zach, who was still waiting for her. "I'm sorry, Zach, I've been rude and unpleasant," she purred.

She climbed on his back and he hoisted her up and began walking. "Do forgive me. I just haven't been myself."

Zach was puffing slightly. "I think you've been very much yourself. More than at other more mysterious times, like this minute."

I've done it, she thought. I've ruined the whole thing. I can see myself taking knitting lessons. No. No. No.

Catherine very gently rested her head on Zachary's shoulder. She nuzzled the side of his neck and then softly blew into his ear. She let one hand touch the side of his face, very slightly.

Suddenly Zachary dropped Catherine from his back. He turned toward her, throwing the flashlight onto the road, and grabbed her shoulders roughly. Then his arms were around her, pulling her close to him, holding her so that she couldn't move . . . if she had wanted to. His mouth covered hers, asking, demanding an answer. His hand moved to hold her face tighly, so that she couldn't turn her head . . . if she had wanted to. Catherine put her arms around his neck and held onto him. The darkness closed in on her until there was only feeling. Warm mouth, strong hands. They clung to each other, swaying slightly, neither one of them moving an inch away. The world was Zachary Winters, nothing else.

When he raised his mouth from hers, he whispered, "It wasn't deliberate, Catherine. I didn't plan this. It's important you believe me."

"I believe you," she answered and kissed him again, moving her mouth from his lips to his cheek and neck. It didn't matter if he had planned it; nothing mattered except that she was more alive than she had ever been before.

Suddenly a car turned into the road, bathing them in headlights. They sprang apart as it stopped and an elderly man got out. "What are you two doing here?" he asked suspiciously.

Zach explained quickly. The man's wife had joined him in the road. "Well, for heaven's sake, Frank, let's take these children to the gas station. Don't just stand there."

Frank looked at his wife and then at Catherine and Zachary. "I don't know. I mean, who knows who they are? We can't take a chance like that."

"Frank," his wife said with exasperation. "Are you just going to leave them here? If they were looking to pick up someone in a car and murder them, would they be on *this* road?"

The couple drove them to the gas station and back to the car with a can of gas that was enough to get them to the station to fill the tank. As Zachary drove Catherine home, she sat close to him, her head on his shoulder. Every now and then he would lean over and rest his head on top of hers. They didn't speak.

On her front porch, she waited for him to say something. Say something, she begged silently. Say you love me or make another date. Something. Something to hang on to. It had nothing to do with the bet. It only had to do with Catherine Dara Farley and Zachary Winters.

He took her in his arms again and kissed her. They had more familiarity with each other now. His mouth was becoming known to her and he knew the softness of her body against his. They were totally gentle with each other, not asking anything, just sharing quick, small kisses, waiting to express the gathering strength of the feelings they had.

The front door opened and Oliver came out. He didn't look at Zachary very long. But he stared at Catherine. Her face, her arms around Zach's neck, her body close to Zach. He narrowed his eyes and went back in.

"Doesn't that kid ever talk?" Zack asked.

"I'm sure he'll have plenty to say soon." Catherine felt a pain go from her toes to her heart.

"I'd better get going," Zach said. "I have another essay on Friday. How about coming over Monday night and helping? I have to be home, baby-sitting with Tommy." He saw Cat hesitate. "Same deal. I mean, I'm not taking advantage. This is a business deal."

Cat smiled. "Sure. I'll be there."

Catherine sat in the porch swing, moving back and forth. She had wanted more. Not just to be asked to help with his essay. She stopped the movement of the swing and lay down on it, curled into a small, tight ball. She closed her eyes. Her feelings seemed too strong to be contained in her body. She sobbed silently, but there were no tears. Then she crossed her arms and clung to herself tightly.

She was in love with Zachary Winters. And more than anything she wanted to lose the bet.

Chapter 8

Slowly, she walked up the stairs. When she got to Oliver's closed door, she paused. She raised her hand to knock, then dropped it.

In her own room, she sank down on the bed. If Zachary knew what she had done, the bet she had made with Tamara, he would despise her. How could he help it? Yet she had to tell him, had to stop the charade . . . if she could. She reached for the phone and then, just as she had dropped her hand at Oliver's door, she withdrew her hand from the phone.

If she told Zach, she would lose him, whatever part of him she had. He wanted an honest girl, and that wasn't Catherine. He wanted a girl like Gina.

She stared at the phone and reached toward it again . . . but she couldn't . . . she couldn't. Suddenly, it rang. *Zach.*

She picked it up and heard Howie's voice.

"Cat? Just wanted to say good-night. My grandmother sends her love to you. I missed you."

Howie's voice was soft, loving. Cat suddenly, without thinking, said frantically, "Howie, listen. . . ." Then she broke off. What was she going to say?

"What is it, Cat? Cat . . . ?" He laughed. "Okay. I'll see you tomorrow night. By then you'll remember what you wanted to say."

Catherine grasped the phone tightly. "Howie, I have to talk to you. Please! Come over."

"Catherine, what's wrong?"

"Howie, you have to come here. Now! Right away! I have to talk to you." She cried silently, tears dripping into the receiver.

"I'll be right there," he said, sounding upset.

She sat in the porch swing and waited the ten minutes it took for Howard to come running up the walk to her house. She pushed the swing back and forth, and felt as if she was barely breathing. She tried to formulate what she was going to say to him, but she could hardly hold onto any connected, sensible thoughts.

All she knew was that she had to tell Howard the truth. Pretending, lying, manipulating had become intolerable and, at the moment, the only person she could try to be honest with was Howard. Maybe then she would like herself a little more than she did.

Maybe then the weight on her chest would lift.

When Howie was at her side, she took his hand and together they went into the house. In the dimly lit living room, she looked at him and tears once again slowly trickled down her cheeks.

"Catherine, what is this all about?" Howie sounded annoyed. "You have to stop the mystery."

"Howie, sit down, please. I can't stand your pacing back and forth."

He sat down and waited for Catherine to say something.

Taking deep breaths, trying to regulate her breathing, she said. "Howie, I . . . I like you a lot. We've had good times together. You're . . . my friend . . . my good friend, but . . . but I don't love you."

Howie laughed gruffly, and stood up. "Is this what this is all about? Catherine, I know you don't love me."

"You do?"

Howard came over and stood looking at Catherine directly for the first time since he had come in. "Cat, do you think I'm such a turkey that I didn't know you don't love me?"

The weight on her chest was still there, almost suffocating. "Of course, I don't think you're a turkey. But why then . . . why have you . . . stayed around?"

The gruff laugh came again. "Easy. Because I'd rather be with you, without your loving me, than not be with you at all."

Catherine sank down into a big easy chair and stared at her hands. Howie came over, knelt down, and took hold of her by her arms. "Okay? Is this all taken care of now? Can I go home and go to bed?"

Catherine shook her head now. "Howard, you should have a girl who loves you, the way you deserve to be loved. That's not me."

Howard put his arms around Cat and hugged her. "Let me decide what I want. Okay?"

Catherine shook her head no again. "There's more, Howard. More. I . . . I'm in love with someone else."

Howard let go of Catherine's arm and stood up. His face contorted once, just once, and then he assumed an almost blank expression. "It's that Winters guy. Isn't it? That's who. Right?"

"Yes," Catherine said, almost imperceptibly.

"Is he in love with you, too?"

Catherine wept softly. "I don't know . . . it doesn't matter. I mean, it doesn't matter between you and me. It has nothing to do with you and me, whether Zach loves *me*. All that matters is that *I* love Zach and I can't be going out with you, lying to you."

Howard was silent.

Cat cried out, "Don't you understand anything that I'm saying, Howie?"

Howard began walking around the room, stopping to punch a pillow or kick at the rug. "All I understand is, it's that crummy, lousy bet. If you hadn't gotten into it with that crazy Tamara, this wouldn't have happened."

"No," Cat said, swiping at her tears with the back of her hands. "It has nothing to do with the bet. It has to do with being honest with you . . . fair to you . . . I never have been . . . really."

Howard looked at Catherine, his face reflecting confusion and anger. "It's the bet."

He walked to the door and Cat ran after him. "Please try not to be angry with me. Try to understand. You'll meet someone else. You'll see. Someone better."

Howard shook his head. "I don't want someone better."

On the porch, Cat pulled on Howard's arm and stopped his movement to the steps. She put her arms around him and held him tightly, not saying anything. Howard's arms reached around Catherine and held her to him . . . for a moment. "I'll talk to you." He ran down the steps and up the street.

Catherine stood and watched him go, hardly knowing what she felt. Then she turned to the front door. A movement in the swing caught her eye and in the dim light she saw Oliver, looking at her. He got up and walked into the house, making sure he didn't brush her arm as he went by her, as if touching her was repellent to him.

Cat reached out for him. "Oliver. Wait! It isn't what you think. Let me explain."

Oliver ran up the stairs, two at a time, and into his room. Cat raced after him, crying all the way, "Wait! Wait!"

She got to his door as it slammed in her face, and she heard the lock turn with a final click.

Catherine banged on the door fiercely, shouting, "Oliver! Let me in! Open the door! Damn you, open the door and let me talk to you!"

She banged with all her strength, weeping as she struck the door with her fists over and over again. Her mother and father came out of their bedroom.

"What the hell is going on here?" Mr. Farley asked angrily.

Pam Farley took a quick look at Catherine and went over to her. "Catherine, come into your room. Stop this yelling and banging."

She led Catherine into her bedroom and sat her down on the bed. She took Kleenex from the bedside table and wiped the tears on Cat's face. Then she took Catherine in her arms and rocked back and forth with her. "There, there. It's all right. Everything will be fine," she crooned softly. "Tell me."

Mr. Farley stood at the bedroom door watching, and then said, "You'd better handle this, Pam. I'm going back to bed. Come in as soon as you can and tell me what's going on."

Catherine clung to her mother and the words came out in short, breathless jerks. Single words . . . phrases . . . tears. "I love

Zach . . . told Howie . . . hates me . . . help. . . ."

Catherine's mother just held her until she stopped crying. Cat stood up and reached for more Kleenex. She shook her head with confusion. "What am I going to do? I love Zach. I want him to know about the bet . . . what I've done. But I can't tell him . . . he'll hate me . . . but I don't want to lie anymore. . . ."

Pam Farley shrugged. "Then you have no choice. You have to tell him and let the chips fall where they may."

"I can't lose him . . . especially since I don't even think I have him."

"Is Zach in love with you?" her mother asked.

"I don't know," Catherine shouted. "Why does everyone keep asking me that? He may be and he may not be. How did I get into this?"

"I told you this bet might not work out the way you thought. People are not puppets that you can just bounce around by invisible strings."

Cat sat on the floor next to her mother and pushed her damp hair away from her face. "Should I tell you what I'm thinking this moment? Should I tell you what your superficial, shallow daughter is thinking?"

"Do."

Catherine jumped up. "I'm thinking that now I don't have a date for tomorrow night. It's going to be Saturday night and I don't have a date. How about that for depth of character?"

Mrs. Farley smiled. "That's not so unusual. People are human. Patients have told me one of the things that they thought of when a person they loved died was what they'd wear to the funeral. So . . . you're not so special."

"Mom, I can't remember the last Saturday night I didn't have a date. I don't even know what girls do . . . when they're alone."

Pam Farley stood up and picked up the wads of wet Kleenex scattered around the room. "I would think you'd call a girl friend. Is there some law of the jungle that says you can't spend a Saturday night with a girl . . . and have a good time, by the way? Try it."

"And Zach. What do I do about him?"

"What do you want to do?"

Catherine walked over to the window and peered out. "I'm going to see him Monday night. I'll tell him then . . . maybe."

Once she was in bed, Catherine tried to sleep, hoping to escape from the conflicting feelings and the fears she had. She felt good because she had confronted Howard; bad, because she was trying to fool Zach. Happy, because she loved Zach; miserable, because Oliver thought she was a crud. She tried to picture herself telling Zach about the bet on Monday night and all it did was make her whimper.

She sat up and dialed Tamara. A groggy voice answered on the third ring. " 'Lo."

"Tamara, it's me. What are you doing tomorrow night?"

"Catherine, have you called me at twelve-thirty to ask me what I'm doing tomorrow night?"

"I have to know."

"I don't know what I'm doing, Cat. I haven't thought about it and I'm certainly not thinking about it now."

Catherine settled back on the pillows. "Okay, whatever you do I'll do with you."

Tamara yawned loudly. "What about Howie? Aren't you going out with him?"

"I broke up with Howie tonight."

Catherine could hear Tamara sitting up in bed and turning on her light. "Why did you do it?"

"I'm in love with Zach and I couldn't not tell Howard."

"Catherine," Tamara shouted. "You can't do that . . . be in love with Zach. You'll louse up the bet."

"Tamara," Cat said with annoyance, "the bet is loused up enough as it is."

Tamara was silent . . . then, "Are you okay? I mean, are you feeling all right? Upset? Not upset?"

"I'm upset and not upset. I'll tell you tomorrow."

Chapter 9

As soon as Catherine woke up the next morning, she knew something was wrong. She felt it in her stomach, in her knotted feet, in her clenched hands. It dropped into her consciousness with a thud. Howie! Howie, and she was alone now. She was one of the girls she used to feel sorry for. Dateless. She would be solitary, lonely, outside of the whole couples flow of school. Couples . . . the magic word. The word that made the difference between in and out.

She jumped up and looked in the mirror. "Oliver's right," she said to her reflection, "You *are* rotten. You have just hurt Howie miserably and all you can think of is yourself."

Yet she knew she had done Howie a favor. Freed him. If only he realized it, she was a liberation army of one.

She showered and poured some orange

juice. The house was quiet, empty. Picking up the kitchen phone, she dialed Tamara. "So what are we doing tonight" she asked dourly.

"What's Zach doing tonight?"

"I don't know. Let's leave Zach out of this for now. Please, what are *we* going to do?"

She heard Tamara turn on her hair blower, and the whoosh of air swept across the streets that separated them. "How about a movie? There's something good at the Empire."

Cat hesitated. "The Empire?"

Tamara turned off the dryer. "You don't want to be seen in town, right? Come on, Cat, join the real world. Take the plunge. Be a girl without a date on a Saturday night for all the world to see. You'll be a better person for it. You'll become a compassionate, high-minded woman. A Florence Nightingale, maybe. An Eleanor Roosevelt."

Cat laughed in spite of herself. Damn Tamara for being so perceptive. "Okay. I'll pick you up at seven."

"Sleep over. Then you can tell me all about Howie and Zach and you. It's a soap opera. *Days of Our Days.* Or, *All Our Teenagers.*"

"Very funny."

On line that night, waiting to buy tickets at the Empire, Catherine looked at Tamara. She was dressed in striped full pants, a red T-shirt, and the flowered, silk jacket they'd bought at the Antique Closet. It occurred to Catherine that Tam didn't dress for the occasion, Tam just dressed. Catherine looked down at the white pants and pink, man-tailored shirt she had on, and felt dowdy. She hadn't thought much about what to wear that night. After all . . . after all, she whispered to herself, cringing, she didn't have a date. How could she have let herself slip into that chauvinist cliche?

Cat looked around her. The usual school kids were also on line. The usual couples clowning around, holding hands, nuzzling each other from time to time, laughing, hug-ging. Catherine watched them, but they didn't look at her. They didn't see her. Heat moved through her, slowly, gathering strength as it progressed up her body. I'm invisible, she thought.

She grabbed Tamara's arm and shook her. "Do you see me? Am I here?"

Tamara pushed Cat's hand off her arm and rubbed the place that Catherine had clutched. "I see you. What's with you?"

"*They* don't. No one has looked at me. They're my friends and they don't see me."

"Lesson two in real life," Tamara said. "They aren't deliberately ignoring you. They — "

Cat interrupted. "I'm just a girl with an-other girl. Right? So I'm not even part of their awareness. I don't penetrate their con-sciousness."

The line started moving and they went inside. Cat bought a jumbo container of pop-corn and stuffed herself throughout the movie. Sublimating. Every time she thought of the kids on line, she shoved another handfull of popcorn into her mouth. At Frascatti's afterwards, she ate half a pizza without stopping to breathe. The restaurant was full, and she watched a lot of the same couples who had been on line at the movie, squeeze into booths and tables at Frascatti's, fitting six where four would have just been comfortable.

Suddenly, she put the slice of pizza down and just stared. Zach was sitting at a table for two with Gina. Gina was crying, as unobtrusively as she could, and he was holding her hand and talking to her gently.

Tamara turned to where Cat's eyes were riveted. "Oh."

Catherine said with shaky vehemence, "Last night he was kissing me. Tonight he's sweeting up to her. What kind of boy is he?"

"You really like him, don't you?" Tamara asked, looking at the hurt expression on Catherine's face.

"So what? So I like him. It's all your fault anyway."

"My fault?"

Catherine glared at Tamara. "Sure, if we hadn't gotten into this ludicrous bet, I never would have had anything to do with Zachary."

Tamara moved drops of Coke around on the table with the end of a straw. "What about the bet? Now you like the guy, it doesn't hold." Tamara looked thoughtful. "Except in reverse."

Catherine pushed at the Coke drops, too. "What do you mean, in reverse?"

"I mean, you like him now, so the reverse holds true . . . you won't get him. I'm sorry, because I want you to have what you want, but truth is truth. . . ."

Catherine sighed. "You really are obsessive . . . and crazy . . . and opinionated . . . and stubborn. That is as much nonsense as the original bet I made with you . . . that I *would* get him because I *didn't* want him."

Tamara smiled. "Want to bet?"

Catherine's mouth tightened and her eyes closed. She threw the wet straw on the table. "Yes. I'll bet. I care about him. I love him. I want him. And I think he feels the same way . . . and he'll show it. I'll . . . I can hardly use the words 'get him,' they are so degrading, but that's what I mean."

"You've got a week and a few days left from our original wager. The clock is going, kid."

Later, in bed at Tamara's, listening to Tam's even, quiet breathing, Catherine thought about the line at the movies. She thought about the hundreds of times she had stood in the same place with Howard. How she had been one of the people laughing and nuzzling. There must have been other girls on line, girls with girls. But she had never been aware of them. She had talked with the girls who were half of a couple, girls like herself. They had compared notes about clothes and parties and school. There had been no other world but theirs. The "in" world, the safe world. The terribly exclusive world where they locked other people out, without even knowing they had a key they were using.

Cat turned on her side, feeling regret, not for the loss of Howard but because she'd never seen Lea Andrews or Marge Cohen or Clare Kazewski when they had stood on line . . . or Tamara? Had she been unaware of Tamara, too? You've got a lot to learn about sisterhood, baby. Okay bet, teach me. I learned to be straight with Howard; what else have I got to get through?

In the morning, Catherine sat up straight in bed. Tamara was sleeping on her back, one hand thrown over her head. Her dark hair was an inky splash on the white pillow.

"Tamara," Cat shouted. She got out of bed and went over to Tam and shook her hard.

Tamara opened her eyes. "Now what?"

"You made me do it again." Cat continued shouting. "I made another bet with you."

Tamara yawned. "It isn't another one, it's the same one, a little different."

"But it's a bet. I'll be in trouble all over again."

Tamara sat up and rubbed her eyes. "Okay, so you lose. It's the end of the bet and I won.

Default is better than nothing."

Catherine got up and went over to the window. She angrily opened the blinds, letting the sun pour in. Tamara blinked and put her hand over her eyes.

"Never," Cat said. "Anyway, I won't feel as guilty about this bet. It's not as dishonest. I want Zachary Winters and I'm going to get him, bet or no bet." But there was a nasty taste in Cat's mouth . . . a taste of losing.

Tamara sank back onto the bed. "It's too early to understand what either of us are saying. Wake me again in a couple of hours." She looked at the clock. "Cat, it's only seven o'clock."

Catherine leaned over and put on her shoes. "I'm going home. I have to clear my head. You're like some kind of magician. You're Houdini or Merlin or who knows?"

"And you're poor Guinevere. Is that it?"

Catherine put on her clothes and stood in the bedroom door. She smiled. "Thanks for last night. I learned a lot."

Tamara smiled back. "I thought you would."

At home, Catherine stood in a hot shower and let the streams of water run over her. She adjusted the sprays to cool, and held up her face to the vitalizing cascade. A voice deep inside said, So lose by default, give up, get out. Don't start this all over again. "No," she said out loud.

She stayed at home that day, did homework, read, made sketches. Oliver avoided her, never looking at her, and Cat gave up trying to reach him. Just once she said to him, "You're a judgmental, cruel child. So some girl hurt you. It happens to everyone. Don't take it out on me."

He didn't answer.

In the afternoon she sat out on the lawn with her mother. Catherine stretched out on the browning grass and let the sun warm her. Her mother was in a chair, reading notes she had made in her sessions.

"How could you have had a boy like Oliver?" Cat asked. "He's mean and unforgiving. Not that I have to explain my actions to a kid."

Pam Farley put down her notes. "He's disappointed. He admired you and he doesn't know how to adjust his feelings."

Cat stayed prone on the grass, her eyes closed. "Just a little more than a week and it will all be over. Then I can talk to him."

Mrs. Farley got down on the grass next to Catherine. "Cat, open your eyes. Look at me! I thought you were through with this. That you were going to tell Zach the truth. What happened?"

"Nothing happened. Now it's an honest bet. We just reversed it. I want Zach, and my bet with Tam is that I can get him. Now I'm not trying to deceive him. I'm just doing the normal, healthy thing, trying to achieve my goals."

"Catherine Dara, it's still a bet. There is still a winner and a loser."

"Right, and I'm going to be the winner."

Cat's mother looked at her. "You're thick or something, Catherine. How much pain do you have to go through to learn?" She got up and went into the house.

Catherine watched her go. She felt a feeling of illness clutch her stomach. As if she might be actively sick.

But she turned her thoughts to Zach, tried to recapture the feelings of Friday night . . . the warm, clinging air, the lights of the amusement park, the feel of his back against her body, and his mouth on hers. The feelings of love.

Then she saw him with Gina at Frascatti's, and the feelings of love turned to feelings of confusion and distrust. Once more illness clutched at her stomach, and she put her hand over her mouth to keep from crying out.

As hard as she tried, she couldn't blot out her mother's words. "You're thick or something. . . . How much pain do you have to go through?"

Why didn't she just give up? Why not tell Tamara the bet was off? She wanted to, so badly she could almost feel the relief of being through with it, out, disentangled. But a gnawing, competitive part of her couldn't allow her to give in to Tamara. It's her certainty, Cat thought. Her unswerving, unquestioning arrogance. She's so sure she's right.

Cat watched the door her mother had slammed closed. She wanted to run after her and say, "You're right. I don't care if I beat out Tam." But she sat on the grass motionless, tears in her eyes.

Chapter 10

The next day she hoped to see Howard in school, and dreaded it. Sitting at the breakfast table, she went over scenarios in her head. What she'd say, what he'd say. She would be mature, calm, soothing. He would be grateful for her strength and benevolence.

But all the while that she was designing her little dramas, she knew that all they were, were make-believe. The pain in her middle told her that clearly.

She was drinking a cup of lukewarm coffee when Oliver came into the kitchen. He poured orange juice and sat down at the table, not in any way recognizing Catherine's presence.

"Oliver," Cat said, trying to be friendly, "we may both live into our nineties. We will be old and white-haired, and will you still not be talking to me? I mean, how long is this going to continue?"

Oliver silently shoveled corn flakes into

his mouth, not raising his eyes from his bowl.

Cat got up from the table, slamming the chair to the floor as she stood up. "Okay. I don't care if you never speak to me again. You're a stupid child."

She ran out of the kitchen, knowing she cared desperately whether he spoke to her or not. She should have tried once more to explain, instead of being flippant. She should have tied him to his chair and forced him to listen to her. Though she had never totally admitted it to herself, and though she certainly had never told Oliver, she loved him. She had been enriched by his unspoken respect for her. It had showed in little, partially hidden ways, and she had always tried to be patient with his unbearable boy-growing-up phases. But now there was nothing between them. No, that wasn't true; if there had been nothing it would have been easier. Now there was undeniable, blatant disgust.

She turned back to the kitchen and stood in the doorway. Oliver raised his eyes to hers, but there was no expression at all. The air between them was dead . . . no emotion of any kind coming from him to fill the vacuum. Catherine turned and walked out of the house.

At school, the first person she saw as she walked down the hall was Howard. She ran toward him and grabbed his arm.

"Howie?"

"What is it, Cat?"

She held on to his arm tightly. "Are you okay? I mean . . . are you — "

Howard took her hand off of his arm. "I'm okay, Catherine."

She bit her lower lip hard. "Would you like to have lunch with Tam and me?" she asked hopefully.

Howard shook his head. "You're bizarre, Cat. No, I would not like to have lunch with Tam and you."

"Howard, can't we at least be friends? I know I hurt you, but it wasn't to be mean. I *had* to tell you."

Howard brushed the hair back from Catherine's flushed face. "I know you didn't want to be mean. There isn't anything mean about you, Catherine, nothing deliberately mean. But . . . maybe someday we can be friends . . . in ten or twenty years, but not now."

He walked away from her, leaving her staring at his slouched figure going down the hall. She went into the ladies' room and into a booth. Leaning against the closed door, she cried as softly as she could without choking. She tried to hold back the bitter sobs that filled her chest. Finally she stopped, washed her face, and went to class.

Staring out of the window, she watched a flock of birds flying in a smooth, constant circle . . . around and around and around. They seemed to have a purpose, as if they knew what they were doing. All of them together, united.

They seemed so calm and purposeful, and I feel so crazy, she thought.

At lunchtime Tamara was at a table before Catherine got to the cafeteria. Cat put her tray down and sat next to Tamara. Tamara picked up the white bread from Catherine's sandwich and peered at the contents. "Catherine, you hate tuna fish. Why did you buy it?"

"Did I buy tuna? I guess I wasn't thinking. I'm not so hungry anyway."

Tamara switched their sandwiches. "Here, I'll eat the tuna and you take my roast beef. You look awful."

Cat picked up the roast beef sandwich silently. Then she said, "I met Howard in the hall. I asked him to have lunch with us, but he said no. Not only that, but he said maybe in ten or twenty years we could be friends."

Tamara put down her sandwich. "Does that surprise you, Catherine? That he didn't think being with us would be a barrel of laughs?"

Catherine sighed. "No, I guess I wasn't surprised. I just think it would be nice if we could at least be friends."

"You want it all, Cat . . . everything your way."

Cat laughed. "Doesn't everybody? I mean, sure I want it all. Why not?"

Tamara shrugged. " 'Cause it doesn't work that way. Nobody has it all. You wanted to be straight with Howard; it made you feel good. So you pay the price. He doesn't feel warm and toasty with you . . . that makes you hurt. Like I said, you can't have it all."

"Don't lecture me, Tamara. I'm not in the mood."

Tamara looked at Catherine quickly, saw the pale face, the drawn mouth, and the brimming eyes. "Sorry. I wasn't lecturing, I was just trying to help."

Catherine took a bite of the sandwich and coughed. Tamara reached over and put her hand over Cat's, her fingers dipping into the ketchup she had put on her sandwich before she had given it to Catherine. "Cat, maybe we should just dump this bet. I mean, you're upset and hurt and — "

Cat stood up, her eyes filled with anger. "Never! Never! I've gone this far. Gone through all the mess and now that I'm sure to win, now you want out. Well, I say *no*. If you want to lose by default, okay."

Tamara jumped to her feet and faced Catherine. "Lose by default? Are you crazed? Never! Okay, the bet is still on."

They stood looking at each other with anger and then, at the same moment, they both giggled. The giggles turned to laughs and then belly laughs; clinging to each other, they filled the entire area with loud, full laughter. Kids at neighboring tables watched them, and then one by one they, too, started laughing, not knowing why. . . . Soon half the cafeteria was laughing. Occasionally someone would ask, "What's funny?" And someone would answer, "Who cares? Don't ask so many questions."

Catherine went up to her room as soon as she got home from school. She intended to do her homework, shower, wash her hair, dress like a dream, eat, and get to Zach's by seven. As she was drying her hair, she heard sounds in Ursula's room and went in.

Ursula was packing some things in a suitcase, not bothering to fold anything, just throwing sweaters, pants, and underwear all in together.

Cat said, "What are you doing here? Don't you ever stay at school where you belong?"

Ursula grinned. "I'm glad to see you, too. Winnie Adams drove over, so I tagged along to bring some stuff back."

Cat nodded and started out of the room. Then she turned. I seem to be doing a lot of this lately, she thought, walking away and turning back. "Ursula," Cat said, "I've fallen in love with Zach and I'm going to tell him about the bet."

Ursula stopped bunching up clothes and tossing them into the bag. "Aren't those two statements contradictory? I mean if you love him, why tell him the truth? The guy will take off like a bat out of hell."

"Ursula, don't you have any common decency? It's *because* I love him that I have to be honest. Don't you understand?"

Ursula sat down on the bed and frowned as she looked at Catherine. "Look, I'm not the right one to talk to about honesty and all that. I'm the girl whose boyfriend was seeing another girl on the sly. Remember? So don't give me that honesty bit."

Cat reached out and touched Ursula's shoulder. "I didn't know. I didn't know that Ben had been dating other girls. I just thought he had wanted some space."

Ursula shrugged and slammed the suitcase shut. "It's not exactly something you brag about . . . that the guy you loved . . . trusted . . . was a no-good cheat. It doesn't do much for one's ego."

"'Do you think I should just not say anything to Zachary?"

Ursula stood up and took the suitcase in her hand. "Would he say anything to you, if things were reversed?"

Catherine thought fleetingly of Gina. "I don't know."

Ursula put down the suitcase and walked over to Catherine. She put her arms around her and hugged her tightly. "Look, to each his own. One woman's meat is another woman's poison. Do what you have to do to live with yourself. In the end, kid, that's the one you have to live with."

Ursula kissed Cat's cheek gently, looking at Catherine's worried, confused expression. "Nobody said it would be easy, Cat."

Ursula walked out of the room, and Catherine reached up to her cheek and brushed away a tear.

After she showered, Catherine went down

to the kitchen to make a sandwich. Her father came home from work before her mother did and started getting dinner ready. As he took a casserole from the refrigerator to put into the oven, he said, "Why the sandwich? You're going to spoil your appetite for dinner."

"I'm not having dinner. I have to be at Zach's by seven."

"Oh, your mother mentioned to me tonight is your moment of truth."

Cat busied herself putting ketchup on her meat loaf sandwich. "I don't know. Ursula says she doesn't see why I have to tell him."

Mr. Farley snickered. "Ursula, the big expert. She's been through more boys in the past two years than I can count."

"Dad . . . if you were a boy, would you want to know about the bet? How would you feel if a girl told you she'd played a game like that?"

Cat's father laughed. "*If* I were a boy?"

"You know," Cat said, "a young man . . . a boy."

"You mean, not decrepit like your old father. Well, let me tell you, there's still a bit of the boy in this guy."

"Dad. Please, be serious."

Mr. Farley's face sobered. "Sorry, Catherine. Let's see. I'd be angry at first, feel manipulated, but I'd also be glad the girl had enough guts and decency to tell me."

Cat took a bite of the sandwich. "Would you hate her?"

"No, I don't think so." Jerry Farley

washed some lettuce for a salad. "Catherine, does this boy, this Zachary, love you?"

Catherine threw down her sandwich. "You, too? *I don't know.*"

"Don't you have a hint? Don't you have any suspicions, one way or the other?"

Catherine poured a glass of milk and sipped it. "I'm not sure. Sometimes, when he kisses me, I get a sense of real deep feeling. You know, real caring under the . . . under the. . . ." Suddenly she was embarrassed.

"Under the passion?" her father asked, clearing his throat nervously.

"Yes." She waited. She'd never talked to her father like this, and they both were feeling a little uncomfortable.

"I guess I'm supposed to be a modern parent and not ask how much you know about passion. But I'm not feeling very modern at the moment, just parental."

Catherine laughed. "I don't know that much about passion. I mean, not the serious part, just the preliminaries."

Catherine's father sighed with relief. "I'm glad," he said, smiling directly at her. "Old-fashioned and glad."

Cat sat down at the kitchen table. "Dad, how come we never talked like this before? How come when I'm crying and distraught, you leave it to Mother and go to bed?"

Mr. Farley sat next to Catherine. "I can't deal with histrionics. Your mother would say I won't, but can't or won't, I feel helpless and stupid, and I don't know what to say or do in situations like that."

"And now?" Cat asked seriously.

"Now we're talking sensibly. No tears, no banging on doors, just talk. I feel I'm reaching the potential adult in you, not the weeping child."

Cat smiled. "Did you ever realize it's okay for grownups to cry, grownup men, too?"

Her father stood up. "You sound just like your mother."

He began dicing carrots, and Catherine knew the discussion was over. For a moment they had touched. Now it was gone. But it had broken the ground and Cat knew there would be other times. She took the plate with the sandwich, and her milk, and started over to the kitchen door.

"Have to get dressed. I'll finish this upstairs."

She left the room aware that her father was watching her go.

Chapter 11

Cat walked over to Zach's, knowing it would be foolish to take her bike, since he would bring her home. She walked briskly, stretching her legs and swinging her arms, enjoying the feel of the soft white T-shirt on her back and the crushed pink cotton pants flowing around her legs. She felt her heart beating faster as she got to his block, and she knew it wasn't from the long walk.

It was still light, but in September twilight came earlier than during the summer months. It would be almost dark soon, and she would miss the long days. There was a light on in Zach's living room. Standing on the porch, the house was silent. She rang the bell and waited.

When Zach opened the door she smiled at him, feeling suddenly shy. He stood in the doorway, not responding to her smile. "I tried to get you on the phone, but you'd already gone."

"Oh," Cat said, uneasy at the cool tone of his voice.

"Yeah. I decided I didn't need any more help with the essays. So I didn't want you to come over."

He stood motionless, looking over her head.

"Okay," Cat said, a sick feeling of discomfort growing in her. "So, let's go to a movie or something."

"I can't leave. My folks are out and I have to stay with Tommy."

"Well, can't I come in? We can just talk or watch tv."

Zach moved from the doorway. "I've got a lot of work to do, so I can't waste much time."

Cat went into the house, trying to understand the coldness in his voice, the stiffness in his body, and his total aloofness from her.

"What's wrong, Zach?"

Zachary walked into the living room and began picking up books, sneakers, magazines that were scattered around. "Nothing's wrong. I'm just busy. Why don't you go home, so you don't waste your time here?"

Catherine felt a combination of anger and fear, but the anger won out. "I'm *not* going to walk home alone. It's almost dark, and my father would have a fit if I walked by myself. You'll just have to put up with me until your parents come home."

"Suit yourself," Zachary said and started upstairs. "I'm going to study."

Fear took over. "Zachary, Friday night we were so . . . so . . . close. I haven't even seen you since then, so I couldn't have said or done anything. So what happened? What changed?" Her voice cracked slightly.

Zachary turned and looked at her, concern crossing his face briefly. Then he just shrugged. "Women! So I kissed you a couple of times. Does that make us a big deal? Come on, Catherine, surely you've kissed guys without marrying them."

"I've kissed a lot of guys," Catherine said loudly. "Forget it. Okay? Go do your work. I'll amuse myself down here."

She turned toward the living room, tears blurring her eyes. She flung herself into a chair and stared at the ceiling. The rotten, lousy boy. The deceptive, uncommitted playboy. And she had worried about being honest with him. That was really laughable. He didn't know what the word honesty meant. What a relief that she hadn't made a fool of herself and leveled with him. What a joke she would have been to him.

She went into the kitchen for a glass of water and looked at the mess. Mrs. Winters should take a course in home economics. Dishes and glasses were on every surface. Pots were in the sink and melting ice cream was on the table. Without thinking, Catherine began putting the dishes into the washing machine. She finished what was in the ice cream container and started washing the pots. The whole family was disgusting, she thought.

Hearing a sound, she looked up. Zach was watching her. "What are you doing?"

"What does it look like I'm doing? I'm cleaning up this mess of a kitchen. Your mother should learn how to — "

"I was supposed to do this," Zach said. "I told my mother I'd clean the kitchen."

Catherine dropped the pot she'd been scrubbing into the sink with a loud clatter. "Well, do take over. This isn't exactly my idea of fun and games."

She went back into the living room and turned on the tv set. She stared at it, not knowing what she was seeing. She was tired, and every muscle in her body seemed to hurt. She'd been stretched so tight for weeks that all she wanted to do was crawl into bed and sleep. And now, tonight seemed more than she could deal with. If she could understand, it would help. But there was nothing she could latch onto and reason through.

Zachary stayed in the kitchen for fifteen more minutes and then walked into the living room. "Look, why don't you call your mother and ask her to pick you up?"

"Are you crazy?" Catherine shouted. "Do you think I want my family to realize I even *know* someone as creepy as you, no less know that someone well enough to offer to help with a crummy essay? And, by the way, since I am forced to waste my time here, I expect to get paid."

"You'll get paid," Zachary shouted back. "Every penny. And then we're square. Right?"

"Right," Cat answered.

Suddenly, Tommy called from his room. "Zach. Hurry. I don't feel well."

Zachary ran up the stairs. Catherine hesitated and then went after him. The kid had sounded so pathetic . . . and sick. Tommy was sitting on the side of the bed. His face was as white as the sheets and his hair was wet with perspiration. Zachary just looked at him. "What's up, Tom?"

Catherine took another good look at Tommy and took his hand. "What's up is what's going to come up in one second."

She pulled Tommy to the bathroom, where he was violently ill. Then she washed his face with a cold wash cloth and gave him sips of water. She said over her shoulder to Zachary, "Get him a clean pair of pajamas."

She went out of the bathroom while Zachary put the pajamas on Tommy. Then she led him back to bed and sat on the edge, wiping his face with the wash rag.

"Feel better?" she asked.

He nodded. "Thanks," he said softly. He reached for her hand. "Will you stay with me a little while?"

Zachary hovered in the doorway.

"You don't have to stay here," Cat said. "You're not much use anyway. Go do your homework or whatever was so important to you."

He left the room and Cat turned the lights off, leaving one small lamp on. She sat holding Tommy's hand. He smiled at her. "You know, you're not as cute as I thought you were. In a pinch, you really come through."

Cat laughed softly. "Thanks. I guess that's a compliment."

"It's supposed to be," Tommy murmured before he fell asleep.

Cat just sat still, looking at his face. The color was coming back. Then she was aware of Zach's voice coming from his room.

"Gina, listen, I got the tickets for the rock concert Saturday night. We lucked out."

Catherine closed her eyes and tightened her lips. She dug the nails of her right hand into her palm, so that she had some physical pain to concentrate on, instead of the ache where she knew her heart must be.

". . . I feel the same way, Gina. Always will."

Rage filled her. Here she was sitting with his sick brother, after staying with the child while he threw up, and the creep was talking to another girl. He was really a degenerate, perverted, everything awful. She gently took her hand out of Tommy's and went into Zach's room.

"I'm going. I'd rather walk home by myself and risk all kinds of mayhem than stay in this house with you one more second. You're despicable. Lowlife of the lowest."

She ran out the door. Zach raced after her. "Catherine, don't be a jerk. You can't go alone. And I can't leave. Just be a grownup and wait until my parents come home."

"Grownup?" Catherine shouted at him. "What would you know about being a grownup? You're a child, a selfish child."

She started walking down the street, then walking faster, and finally began running. She fled down street after street. Quiet streets. Dogs barking at her. Cars, the few there were out, slowed down so the drivers could look at the beautiful blond girl racing down the street, her hair flying around her face, not quite covering the tears that ran down her cheeks. It was hard to breathe, and her nose was running. She wiped it on her sleeve as she ran through the streets. She kept muttering, mean . . . mean . . . mean . . . rotten . . . rotten.

She burst into her house and up the stairs. Her mother and father had been sitting in the living room and both of them came out as she ran up the stairs.

"You're early, aren't you?" Pam Farley asked.

"No. Not early enough. Much too late, in fact." Cat went into her room and slammed the door shut.

In a few seconds there was one tap on the

door and Cat's mother came in. "*What* is up?"

Cat was lying on her bed, rigid, her fists clenched, her eyes closed. "I've been had."

Pam Farley sat in the chair near the bed and looked at Catherine. "I thought Zach was the one who was had."

Catherine opened her eyes and rolled over to face her mother. "Well, you thought wrong. He is really a terrible boy, Mother. After being loving and dear and caring Friday night, tonight he was cold, rude, nasty — even called Gina on the phone while I was there. And that after I cleaned up the filthy kitchen and held his head while he threw up."

"Zachary threw up?"

"Mother, you're not listening. Tommy threw up."

"I'm listening, Catherine. You're not communicating. Start from the start."

And Catherine did. When she had finished Mrs. Farley was silent. "It's strange, that's true. I don't understand him."

Catherine stood up and started brushing her hair, violently, pulling at it harshly. "What's to understand? He's just a Casanova type. Surely you've heard of those in your years of practice. He's a guy on the make. Simple."

Catherine's mother took the brush from Cat's hand and put it back on the dresser. "No need to be bald before your time, Catherine," she said. "I don't think he's a Casanova.

I don't know what he is, but I think you're wrong."

Catherine began taking off her clothes and reached into the closet for her pajamas. "Can you imagine if I had 'confessed' to him? What luck that I hadn't."

As she fumbled with the buttons on her pajama top, she started sobbing. Throwing herself in her mother's arms, she said between sobs, "The awful thing is, I still love him. The whole thing is over before it even began."

Mrs. Farley tucked Catherine into bed and kissed her forehead. "Try to sleep. Don't think anymore. Sleep."

After her mother left the room, Catherine thought, How did this happen?

Chapter 12

Catherine drifted through her classes the next morning. She didn't even try to concentrate on what was happening. Her head was filled with the night before . . . the strangeness, the hurt, the unhappiness. Most often she heard Zachary's voice saying to Gina, ". . . feel the same way, Gina. Always will."

Always will . . . what? Love her, of course. What else could those words mean? And she had given up Howard for a boy in love with another girl. But one thing had nothing to do with the other. She had been right about Howard. Lonely as she felt now, she had done the decent thing.

At lunchtime, Catherine went into the cafeteria, eager to talk to Tamara. She saw her immediately at a large table with five other girls around her. Tamara waved to Catherine and pointed to an empty chair next to her. Cat shook her head no, and started for the door. She couldn't. She couldn't make pleasant conversation, put meaningless words together today.

Tamara ran across the room and grabbed Catherine's arm. "What's wrong? Come on and have lunch with us."

"I can't. I have to talk to you alone. Later. After school. We'll go to my house."

"Catherine, tell me what's wrong."

"Later, Tamara. Don't bug me."

Catherine went outside, buying an apple and a container of milk on her way. She sat under a tree on the lawn that surrounded the school, and took out her sketchbook. Slowly, she sketched a restaurant that teenagers would be happy and comfortable in.

As she worked she lost herself. Zachary was almost gone; Howard was almost gone. All there was, was her pad and pencil and the ideas that spun through her brain. She smiled slightly as she worked, stopping to bite into the apple, drink the milk. The hour passed and it was time for afternoon classes.

Tamara and Catherine took the bus home together, but Catherine refused to talk about anything serious until they were at her house.

"I think you're just trying to irritate me," Tamara said.

"Not so. I just don't want to bare my intimate life with who knows who sitting behind us, listening."

"There are two twelve-year-olds behind us," Tamara said.

"Yeah, well they have ears, too," Cat said stubbornly.

When they got home, Catherine brought Cokes and pretzels and potato chips out onto the porch. They sat in the big rockers and finally Catherine said, "I was at Zach's last night and he practically threw me out as soon as I got there. He was nasty and cold and totally uninterested in me."

Tamara looked disbelieving. "Why?"

Cat shrugged. "I have no idea, but he obviously doesn't went to see me, talk to me, or have me in his life in any way."

"I don't understand."

"Well," Cat said. "You were right. I want him and I'm not going to get him. You win, I guess. What kind of muffins do you want?" Catherine hunched dejectedly in the rocker, moving back and forth.

"Catherine, are you just going to give up like that? Not put up a fight? I mean, are you a quitter?"

Catherine stopped rocking. "Tamara, what do you want from me? I'm tired and hurt and confused, and I just want all this to end. Okay?"

"No," Tamara said firmly. "You say you love this guy. So are you going to let one night when he was rotten end the whole thing? If you want him, go after him."

"Love," Cat repeated. "It's such a funny word. I say I love him but I hardly know him. Love is for life, and I may not want Zach for life. We use the word love so freely."

Tamara was annoyed. "Okay! Okay! So we say love when we mean physical attraction, interest, concern. But so what? Don't cop out with semantics. If you think you love Zach, whatever that means to you, fight for him."

"Tamara, you didn't hear. I said I lose the bet. You win."

Tamara got up and knelt next to Cat's chair. "This isn't about the bet, Cat. This is about you and what you want. You're my friend. I don't like seeing you pale and hurting. The hell with the bet. What do you want?"

Catherine was silent for a while. "What should I do?"

Tamara thought and then said, "Go talk to him. Make him tell you what is going on in his head. Ask him . . . does he care about you? Does he love Gina? What about all the kisses and hugging stuff?"

"He said that meant nothing."

"Make him put it in writing."

The next day after school, Catherine went to the Come and Get It. She waited for two hours, watching everyone who came and went. But Zach was not one of them. The longer she waited, the clearer it became that this was a dumb move on her part. What could they possibly say to each other in the middle of a crowded restaurant? She would have to come up with something more logical.

After three cups of tea, one English muffin,

and a dish of ice cream, she left. She was glad to escape; unwilling, if she was honest with herself, to confront Zach . . . and to know whatever they had had was no longer in existence.

At home, she called Tamara. "He didn't come to the coffee shop."

"So you'll have to try something else," Tamara said.

"Like?"

"Like, beard the lion in his own den. He can't run away there."

Catherine moved the receiver from one ear to another. "You mean go to his house?"

"Exactly."

"Tamara, you are crazed. I can't do that. His parents will be home. Tommy is there. I would be humiliated beyond belief."

"Catherine, are you going to spend the rest of your life hanging around the Come and Get It? You'll be arrested for loitering and get fat in the process."

"Tamara, I'm hanging up. Talking to you just gets me into trouble."

At dinner, Catherine played with her food, but didn't really eat. She saw her mother and father exchange questioning glances over her head. Oliver, as usual, didn't look at her at all.

Suddenly she got up and pushed her plate away from her. She threw her napkin on the table and said, "I have to go out for a while. I won't be long."

"Where are you going?" Pam Farley asked.

"I have a lion to beard."

"Catherine Dara," her father called after her as she ran out the door. "What is all this about lions?"

She got on her bike and rode as fast as she could to Zachary's house. She kept repeating herself, "Don't change your mind. Don't change your mind. Keep going."

At his door, she leaned against it for a moment, catching her breath, building up her courage, running her fingers through her hair. Finally, she rang the bell.

Mrs. Winters came to the door. "Oh, you're that Farley girl who baby-sat once. Can I help you with something?"

"I'd like to see Zachary, please." Her voice cracked slightly and she cleared her throat.

"Come in. He's upstairs. I'll call him." Mrs. Winters looked puzzled, but didn't ask any questions.

Suddenly, Zachary was there beside his mother in the hall. "What do you want, Catherine?"

"Obviously, I want to talk to you."

Zachary turned away from her. "Look, I'm busy and I don't have the time to talk."

Mrs. Winters looked at Zachary with surprise. "Zachary, you're being rude. If Catherine wants to talk to you, certainly you have a few moments to spare."

"Ma, keep out of this. Please."

"Zachary," Catherine said, her voice rising. "I'm not going to leave this house until you talk to me. If I have to stay here forever, I will."

"Zach," Mrs. Winters said nervously, eyeing Catherine with concern, "talk to her."

Zachary looked at Catherine for a moment, but there was no expression on his face that Catherine could gather any insight from. "Okay, come up to my room."

Catherine remembered the first time she had stood in Zach's room . . . it seemed so long ago. The room held the smell of his aftershave, the bed had the imprint of his body, and even his dirty socks in a corner moved her.

"Okay," he said, "what do you want to say?"

"Zachary, what happened? Tell me what happened and I won't bother you again. I can't stand not knowing."

Zachary was impassive. "Nothing happened. You imagined a lot that wasn't there. It's that simple."

Catherine snapped. The smell of his lotion, and standing close to him in his bedroom, and the look of the mouth that had kissed her tenderly, passionately, all evoked feelings in her. She loved him, hated him, and was enraged at him. Impassivity was more than she could bear.

"You're a creep," she shouted. "What a mistake I made falling in love with you. Whatever love means. And to think the first time I saw you when I said to Tamara that you weren't my type — that started this whole damn thing. She had to take me up on that. Okay, so I was rotten, too. I made the dumb bet. I bet her that she was wrong, because she said I could get you because I didn't want you, and I said I *couldn't* get you just because I didn't want you. So I was rotten, but you are just as rotten."

"I know," Zachary said, interrupting her.

"You don't know anything at all. You are just macho, unfeeling — "

"I know," he repeated and came over to Catherine. He took her by the arms and shook her, looking into her eyes.

"Know what?" Cat asked.

"I know about the bet."

Catherine pushed his hands away and sank down on the bed. "You *know*? How?"

Zachary stood over her, looking down. "Oliver called and told me."

"Oliver!" Catherine cried out. "My own brother a stoolie?"

"He felt he had to. He called Monday and told me. Try to understand his point of view. You disappointed him terribly . . . so he turned on you. You disappointed me, too, and I'm angry and I feel deceived. I cared about you and I . . . well, I wanted you to tell me the truth. Wanted you to care enough about me to level with me. I hoped you would."

Catherine tried to keep her voice steady. "I . . . I wanted to. I didn't mean to deceive you. I didn't know *you* when I started. . . . It wasn't like I was manipulating Zachary Winters. You were just some strange boy in the garden. Then, when my feelings changed — "

"What about Monday night? You could have told me then. I waited for it," Zach said tightly.

Catherine pushed her hair from her forehead. "But you were so awful to me, from the moment I walked in. How could I say anything to you then?"

Zachary looked at Catherine coldly. "I was awful for good reason. You could have been honest, no matter what. It didn't have to be *easy* for you to be straight. But you chose not to. You made the choice, Catherine."

Zachary turned away and began putting the papers on his desk into neat piles, never looking up.

"Zachary, please forgive me. I'm really not like that. I *am* honest. I never meant any of this to happen. I never meant to hurt anyone."

"I forgive you, Catherine. Okay? Satisfied?"

"And that's all?"

"What else do you want? That's it."

Catherine turned and walked to the door. She concentrated on keeping her head high. There were no tears now, no sobs. Just painful breathing. She had to force her feet to take the steps out of his room . . . out of his life. One in front of the other, one in front

141

of the other. She wanted to turn and run to him, to beg him to love her. To throw her arms around his neck and not let go. But she moved slowly to the door, trying not to stumble. The room was so quiet she could hear her footsteps.

Catherine went downstairs, not hearing Mrs. Winters calling out to her as she walked out the front door. She got on her bike and pushed it out onto the road. Hardly able to lift her legs, she got on and started pedaling. She never rode at night and it frightened her. She concentrated fiercely on the road, on the cars that went by, on stopping at each corner and looking carefully right and left. She hoped her tail light was bright enough, and tensed as every car approached her. Perspiration trickled down her neck and sides and made her shiver in the cool night. Her hair clung damply to her face and her palms were sweating. She watched the streets go by, aching to be home.

Suddenly a car was right alongside her. She glanced at it out of the corner of her eye, not wanting to switch her focus from directly ahead of her.

"Catherine," Zachary called out. "Please stop. You can't ride in the dark." His voice was unsteady.

She never took her eyes off the road. "I'll be home soon. I don't need your help. I'm all right."

"*I'm* not all right," Zach said. "Cat, stop riding and talk to me."

"Go away, Zach."

"Catherine, stop," he shouted, angrily.

She stopped riding, surprised by the tone of his voice, and Zach immediately pulled up to the side of the road. He jumped out of the car and lifted Catherine off her bike, pulling her and it to one side. She was leaden in his arms, but he dumped the bike on the ground and held her tightly against him.

"Cat. Cat, I love you. You did tell me the truth before, and I just was so . . . so unbending . . . stubborn."

He kissed the side of her face, and her hair, and her neck. She hung on to him and hugged him as tightly as she could.

"Zach. I didn't mean to hurt you or anyone. I didn't."

He picked her up and carried her to the car and then put the bike in the back. In the front seat they clung together, terrified at how close they had come to parting.

Cat began kissing him again and then stopped. "Wait! What about Gina? She's your girl, isn't she?"

Zach laughed. "No. We grew up together. We've been friends since kindergarten."

"But I've seen the way you are with her, holding her hand, brushing away her tears, talking so sweetly to her. What's that all about?"

"Catherine, Gina is getting over a rotten romance, where the guy was pretty insensitive to her. I'm just there to help. To build her morale. That's it."

Catherine thought about it. "And what about 'I feel the same way, Gina. Always will.' What did *that* mean?"

"You're an eavesdropper as well as a bet-maker. What am I getting into?"

"Zachary, I was sitting with your brother who had been sick and I couldn't help hearing you. You talk loud sometimes."

"Okay. She said she hoped we'd always be friends, no matter what happened to us. And I said, Miss Big Ears, 'I feel the same way. Always will.'"

Catherine looked out of the car window. "I'm sorry, Zach. I like Gina. I hope she'll be my friend, too . . . I think."

Zachary pulled Catherine back to him. "Come on. I'll take you home. I can't take any more emotional upheavals. But first. . . ."

He took her in his arms and kissed her, gently, sweetly.

They drove home in silence. Catherine rested her head on the back of the seat and let herself drown in the nearness of Zach. Once he reached over and put his hand on her knee.

On the porch of her house, he pulled her down onto the swing and kissed her deeply. She held onto him with all her strength and he hugged her to him.

Then he stood up, pulling her with him. He kissed her once more, deeply. Catherine leaned against him, weary and drained. "I'll call you tomorrow," he said, and ran down the walk. At the bottom, he turned and waved to her, smiling a smile that made her heart turn over.

She pushed the door open and went into the house. Oliver was sitting at the bottom of the stairs. He had obviously heard and seen everything . . . again. His face was white and his brown eyes wide and confused.

Catherine sat on the step next to Oliver. "I know you told Zach . . . about the bet. I guess I understand why you did it. I mean . . . Mimi and all that . . . and more . . . us."

Oliver was silent, his hands clenched.

Tentatively, Cat reached out and touched the clenched hands. "I didn't mean to hurt anyone, Oliver. I know I did, but I didn't mean to."

"That night," Oliver said, "on the porch. First you kissed Zach, then Howie. Dangling two guys. Both nice guys. What kind of girl does that? Tell me."

"No," Cat shouted. "That night when I was with Howie . . . it wasn't what you thought. I had told him about Zach. I was just saying good-bye to Howie. That's all!"

Oliver stared straight ahead. "Still. Still," he said, "to make a bet about getting a guy. It stinks."

Cat felt tears fill her eyes. "I know that. Now forgive me, Oliver. Please. I didn't mean to hurt Howie or Zach or you."

For the first time in a long time, Oliver looked at Cat directly. He saw her tight face and the tears, and he sighed from deep inside himself. He stood up. "I don't understand," Oliver said. "I don't understand a lot of things. I'm going to bed. I'll see you tomorrow."

Catherine knew it wouldn't help to say anything more. She watched him walk up the stairs, his shoulders slumped.

"Oliver," she called out.

He turned and looked down at her.

"I love you, Oliver." She whispered it. But he heard.

Up in her room, she lay on the bed with the lights out. Oliver would forgive her, eventually. She knew that. But she knew, too, he would never feel exactly the same about her. But she would never feel exactly the same about herself, either.

And Howie . . . he'd recover, too, but she had hurt him. Would he ever be her friend again? Probably not. You don't feel very friendly to someone who dumps you. Tamara would say, You win some, you lose some.

Just a simple, innocent bet had caused so much anguish. Cat turned on the light and dialed Tamara. When Tamara picked up the phone, Cat said, "I just want to wind this up, and then I don't think I ever want to talk about it again."

"What happened?"

"I went to Zach's, like you said, and we worked things out. He loves me, and he forgives me. At least he says he does, which is more than Oliver is saying. It's a happy ending for Zach and me? Right?"

"Right," Tamara said.

Cat laughed a stiff laugh. "You know, what should be a *great* happy ending isn't all so totally happy."

"Nothing is," Tamara said.

Catherine rolled onto her back and stared at the ceiling. "You knew that. I didn't."

"Live and learn," Tamara said, but gently, lovingly.

Then Tamara laughed . . . and was silent. "I guess that means you won the bet. You wanted him . . . and you got him."

"I never thought about it," Cat said. "But now that you mention it I did win . . . with your help."

"Okay, Catherine, so I'm your servant for *two weeks* since, as you pointed out, I *did* help. What do you want?"

Catherine sat up and thought for a moment. "Only one thing."

"What?"

"I want you to promise me you'll never make another bet with me for the rest of our lives."

"That's it?" Tamara asked. "That will be the only thing you ask of me?"

"Right," Cat answered.

"You've got it, I promise."

"Fine," Cat said.

Tamara giggled and said softly, "I bet I don't keep the promise."

About the Author

Ann Reit has been an editor of young adult novels for over ten years. She is the author of seven books for young adults, including *Yours Truly, Love Janie,* and *Phone Calls*. Ms. Reit lives and works in New York City.

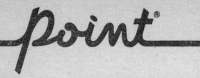

Other books you will enjoy,
about real kids like you!